Eden, Ohio

ALSO BY SHAWNE JOHNSON

Getting Our Breath Back

Eden, Ohio

SHAWNE JOHNSON

DUTTON

DUTTON
Published by Penguin Group (USA) Inc.
375 Hudson Street, New York, New York 10014, U.S.A.
Penguin Books Ltd, Registered Offices: 80 Strand,
London WC2R 0RL, England
Penguin Books Australia Ltd, 250 Camberwell Road,
Camberwell, Victoria 3124, Australia
Penguin Books Canada Ltd, 10 Alcorn Avenue,
Toronto, Ontario, Canada M4V 3B2
Penguin Books (N.Z.) Ltd, Cnr Rosedale and Airborne Roads,
Albany, Auckland 1310, New Zealand

Published by Dutton, a member of Penguin Group (USA) Inc.

First Printing, February 2004
10 9 8 7 6 5 4 3 2 1

REGISTERED TRADEMARK—MARCA REGISTRADA

Library of Congress Cataloging-in-Publication Data

Johnson, Shawne.
    Eden, Ohio / by Shawne Johnson.
        p. cm.
    ISBN 0-525-94810-4 (hardcover : alk. paper)
1. Fugitive slaves—Family relationships—Fiction. 2. African
American neighborhoods—Fiction. 3. African American families—Fiction.
4. Ohio—Fiction. I. Title.
    PS3610.038E24 2004
    813'.6—dc22   2003016642

Printed in the United States of America
Set in Sabon

*In memory of Shanel LaRae Johnson
and Brian Stephen Johnson*

Eden, Ohio

Chapter One

A fine drifting line separated the ground from sky. The ground was dark with life and purpose, sky clear glass, no clouds on the horizon or variations of color, pure blue spanned out into forever. Dark earth and pure blue spanning out into forever called forth life, moving creatures with warm blood beneath the skin, flying creatures with gilded wings, great whales and small fish swimming through unpolluted waters. All of it was blessed to multiply.

Generations and generations later a small part of green things and dark earth was still thriving. Trees were full figured and lush, leaves so healthy bright skin slick when runaway slaves first settled in a large grassy clearing and named their piece of the world Eden. Runaway slaves made a home out of earth waiting to be tilled and forests waiting to be cut down and animals waiting to be hunted and fish in the lake waiting to be caught. They built homes and communities, gave birth to children, watched dreams of safety and plenty gather substance, not float beneath the conscience like shadows. There were no white people at all, just descendants of slaves with glowing dark skin. History written down in books for public school children skipped over that small part of the world where magic was still possible and beauty not out of the ordinary.

Skipped over Eden.

In the early 1980s, grass ankle- to knee-high in Eden, in some places trampled by children's feet and other places cut down by roaring and greedy lawn mowers. Only the really stubborn persisted in mowing grass, dragging huge heavy equipment in summer heat to the edge of town, cutting at wildness that only grew back quick, strong, and lush. Green things growing a perfect home for birds in trees hidden by foliage; squirrels and possums and badgers and mice running freely, carelessly across the green grass floor.

People in Eden used to waking up, looking outside their windows and seeing trees reaching for sky during summer, grass thick and soft like a vain woman's hair, earth rich and sweet like devil food's cake or just-baked bread. The highway leading to town cut a man-made path through the green on the east and west, the only break in nature, and nature constantly threatened to push up concrete and guard rails, leave nothing but weeds and wildflowers. Eden tucked away, no one's destination, no tourist's town with sights and four-star restaurants and crowded streets. Eden a place to come from, a place in the blood of people, hidden like jewels or lepers, a place familiar and loved and lived in or not known at all.

Cities like New York and Philadelphia and Chicago had founding fathers and old streets and homes. Eden was founded by a woman, never written about, everything old and rarely changing. The children left for college and careers and sweet-tongued men or sly smiling women, but they came back with husbands and wives and babies. The children of Eden had a rhyme that they sang jumping rope, skipping hopscotch, playing tag:

Eden, Ohio

On this land I was born
Free not a slave
On this land I will die
Singing free to my grave

There were no words written down in history books, but anyone born in Eden or moved to Eden by husbands and wives who couldn't sleep at night in any other city, in any other small town without dreaming about the lush green surrounding Eden and full-figured trees reaching for blue skies, knew Eden's story by heart. Husbands and wives who fell from sleep with weeping hearts knew the story passed from mother to daughter and father to son.

There were twelve first families in the year 1860, skin brown and blue black and deep red and high yellow. They walked fast through thorny underbrush with only the stars to guide, the moon to give light. Branches scratched at skin, left tender bloodred welts, bare feet swollen and bruised, soles hard and callused. Bare feet the slightest cushion from ground scattered with broken twigs, fallen acorns, nasty-ripe animal shit. They walked in the dead of night because sun in the sky too dangerous, sun in the sky meant people on the roads, people with guns and whips and fast horses and well-built wagons. People looking for blue black and brown and high yellow and deep-red bodies. That's all they were during long walks that started in North Carolina and ended in Eden, bodies to work, to beat. Nothing they had, not even their own feet and hands and eyes and mouths, belonged to them until map of stars and light of moon led them out the belly of the whale.

That long walk was beyond exhausting, beyond working in the fields from sunup to sundown with the sound of the whip circling, beyond working in the big house and being available to anyone all the time. They hid by day and walked in bodies not theirs by night. They were nothing more than haunts, never seen, only traces and tracks and strange noises from exhaustion to scare children, safe in bed with parents nearby, to sleep. Some of them had their own children, babies still young enough to be at the breast, but most of their children gone, never theirs, just bodies as well. Mamas with babies kept them quiet with breast milk and makeshift warmth. Babies, serious, wide-eyed, patient and waiting, picked up on all the fear and determination in the air like mist after summer rain.

The farther and farther they got away from North Carolina and lash falling and fear always sitting in the gut like links and links of steel chains the more they became themselves. No masters or mistresses lurked about, no spoiled, cruel children with far too much power and not enough sense. No getting up at the light of day and lying down with the moon high in night sky. No lashes waited to dig and carve in flesh made rough by years and years of work. Their hands were their hands, and their mouths their mouths, their eyes and noses and ears and feet all theirs. For the first time they were more than only slaves.

The first full day of the long journey the worst, they walked through the dark and familiar objects like trees and sounds, houses in the distance, and the calls of night owls a horror. All of them listened hard for the bark and snarl of dogs giving chase. Only one of them not nervous, not listening, the woman who had gotten them all together, convinced them freedom possible. Eliza was calm leading them out of darkness, praying softly under her breath, so soft prayer sounded like gentle hum, the kind of hum used to lull babies to sleep. Her infant daughter strapped to her back and Eliza repeated Bible verses memorized from Psalms:

*Who shall ascend into the hill of the Lord? or who shall
stand in his holy place?*
*He that hath clean hands, and a pure heart; who hath not
lifted up his soul into vanity, nor sworn deceitfully.*
*He shall receive blessings from the Lord, and righteous-
ness from the God of his salvation.*

Eliza was a magic woman, magic in her family passed
down from mother to daughter since before memory, strong
magic, magic to reshape the world. Eliza took care of the
dogs, took care of those who might have betrayed them,
guided the path that they followed and nobody asked her
how or why, magic as ordinary as brutality, a gift from the
Lord like fresh water to drink and good food to eat.

Some died along the way, no time for burial, just time
enough to murmur quick prayers and keep on moving.
Death was common and nothing to fear. Men with backs
bent from work and women with marks from the lash lining their backs and breasts and thighs sought death out,
looked for death each time the lash fell.

Death was easy, not like living day in and day out and
hoarding all the small joys because no big joys were coming
along. Small joys like holding a baby before they took her
away, lying with lovers under full moon and laughing stars before they were sold downriver. No big joys like watching and
nurturing a child from cradle to grave or holding a lover forever or at least until arms grew heavy and tired. Small, small
joys left the heart aching and wanting more, never quite full.

Ohio waited for them like home always waits, never
really changes—large clearing surrounding by looming, ancient trees and wildlife scurrying and sun high in the sky, waters of the great lake nearby. All that beauty just waited for
them. The first baby cried when they walked into that clear-

ing, cried after weeks and weeks of being silent and still and afraid and the sound closer to long, easy laugh. Long, easy laugh of the cry chased birds from tree branches and sent field mice and harmless snakes racing back into ground.

First twelve families settled, raging exhaustion making it almost impossible to go any farther. And there was no way to walk away from that land. Land far enough away from other cities and towns that they felt safe. Land green and soil dark and moist and smell in the air like life, like smell of newborn child just from the womb. Land wild and abundant and free unlike the place they ran from, a place where land gobbled up and cultivated and never theirs.

There were no families really on the secretive walk up through the South. Just men and women, some with babies, who maybe knew each other or maybe didn't. Families hard to keep together in North Carolina when at any moment anyone was capable of disappearing, vanishing like cooking-fire smoke right into thin air. The green of land all theirs to work like a mating call, pulled them close to each other, bodies belonging now only to them the very best kind of aphrodisiac.

A few years later came the Civil War and the Emancipation Proclamation. By the end of the war first twelve families settled into Eden, Eden theirs to nurture, theirs to protect, theirs to love. The love came easy, so much love inside for what was theirs just waiting during long, never forgotten years as chattel. No white people found Eden those first years, almost as if Eden a place that existed only in slave spirituals, most of which white people didn't think were worth knowing. Slaves free at last all across the country and more black yellow brown red people, exhausted and beaten down and hopeful, stumbled into Eden, stumbled through all the lush green surrounding the clearing and found, unexpectedly, home.

Chapter Two

In the year 1885, all of Eden knew they were blessed, worked the soil with tender hands and a calm in the breast. They had children and babies flourished. No babies died in childbirth or from childbirth fever, accidents that left deep cuts open and bleeding in child-soft skin, falls that knocked children unconscious for long minutes. The crops grew, the children grew, everywhere life and more life. They were fruitful, multiplied, replenished the earth and subdued it. In Eden, the blessings bountiful, never stopped, blessings so plentiful they were soon overcome with gluttony. Bellies full and children safe and lovers free enough to actually love and not just go through empty motions and they forgot aching hunger of not having enough, being enough, fear always in the belly making it impossible to digest any part, miniscule or huge, of life.

Eliza, the daughter of Eliza who brought twelve families out of the dark into the light, watched Eden grow full from having too much, fullness so rich and satisfying that they took it for granted, became lazy and, worse, unthankful. Eliza grew right along with Eden since the founding of the town by her mama. Eliza and Eden were the same age, twenty-five easy years. She took care of the town, took care of the people just like her mother until she found her final peace in Eden's graveyard. The same way her infant daughter would take care of the town—it was in their name, in their blood, in the responsibility of being the firstborn girl.

No matter what the people of Eden did or didn't do, vegetable and flower gardens lush and vibrant, livestock healthy and chicks and calves strong and abundant, infants at the breast clear eyed and safe. Eliza had her mama's magic passed from mother to firstborn daughter since beginning of time and first glare of heavenly light. Eliza watched Eden drown in plenty, tried to head off the inevitable, gave each household herbal teas to rid well-fed, content bodies of laziness, gave each household sweet-smelling herbal salves to rub into the skin and rub out ungratefulness. Eliza too late, guilty of the same gluttony overtaking the town, by the time she sensed something not quite right, no magic strong enough to make any kind of difference.

No way to pinpoint when or how the unimaginable happened, no way to figure out when the first person slept and awakened without, habitually, giving thanks, when the first child was allowed to slide into bed next to warm bodies belonging to brothers and sisters without singsong rhyme falling from well-kissed, good-night mouths.

Eden stopped praying, stopped asking, stopped needing, took for granted all their flourishing and abundant gifts.

Eliza, daughter of Eliza who led them out the wilderness, waited, horrified because no way to force people to give thanks if they were unthankful, willful, greedy children. Punishment was the only sensible answer. She held her infant daughter close to her, put her in the bed with her and her husband, Joseph, at night. Her infant daughter shared her name, shared her face, and history. Eliza looked at her baby in deep sleep and knew real fear.

Eliza waited for punishment, tried to cushion the blows. She watched new babies carefully to make sure hearts beating properly and breath coming easy, watched crops and livestock to make sure nothing rotten and vile in the earth or bloody in full animal bellies. Eliza worried and looked in all the wrong places. She was absolutely stunned when the first white person hacked through the green surrounding town and offhandedly and arrogantly laid claim to what certainly was not theirs.

The rest of Eden didn't recognize the danger, isolated for a generation and slavery twenty plus years abolished and black people free. They didn't run white people out of town and they weren't welcoming. They tolerated, easy lives of plenty convinced them there was enough. Eliza drew protective circles with white chalk around homes, placed drops of protective oil on the foreheads of every man, woman, child. Black people smiled at her, sat still for her, the daughter of the first Eliza. But she could not banish dangerous complacency, slept at night with vicious nightmares crowding her head and forming circles and circles of thick, white smoke around her heart.

A town settled by black folks, descendants of slaves, the same as a town that didn't really exist for most white people. White people with gold red dark flowing hair and green blue hazel eyes, rainbow colored eyes that childishly willed black folks, with the best acres of land and well-tended homes and gardens, to vanish. When wishing and willing failed miserably, rainbow colored eyes narrowed and people with red dark gold flowing hair turned murderous.

Late night and white mist covered Eden like a death

shroud and Eliza sat on the porch of her cabin trying to make white mist—all the time smothering her in dreams and making breath impossible—part. Like Moses parted turbulent waters, but her people already fallen from favor and magic without divinity no magic at all, nothing more than children's tricks. Her baby daughter was inside sleeping next to Joseph in their bed, covers pulled high over them both. The night so quiet Eliza wondered how anyone slept at peace in soft beds without monotone hum of crickets and shrill, comforting sound of night owls, and whisper of soft furry things moving through the dark. She thought of her mama buried and resting in the green, felt Mama's hands moving over her head like she was a little girl again and Mama trying to calm her down, brace her to face whatever was to come.

Bright afternoon sun rose in the distance, rose in dark night sky with hanging bloodred moon, startled her, hands grabbed for her chest and her mouth fell open slow. Daylight came early to Eden and the brightness of the sun and bloodred hanging moon illuminated lushness of the green surrounding Eden—wet and shiny leaves, flourishing gardens, deep blue black earth.

Then came smoke, thick and black and smelling like quick to catch fire vegetation, wood, homemade clothing, bodies. Eliza fell from her porch, scraped knees and elbows and the palms of hands, didn't feel it, gained her footing, kept running, scream one long continuous prayer leaping from her throat. Candles lit in houses behind her, doors thrown open, people stared at her, gaped at sun looming larger and larger in nighttime sky.

Men on horses rode fast and laughed into nighttime air, laugh obscene and white faces wet from heat and viciousness. They almost ran her down, her body lifeless and ashes to ashes and dust to dust. Eliza knew, long before she reached the two neighboring fiercely burning houses, that there were no survivors, nothing living, two families just gone the way Mama told her folks suddenly and unexpectedly vanished into night air during slavery, no bodies at all left to bury.

Nothing to do but watch, watch smoke and ashes dance, ride up in burning flames, think about the children, nine in all, from both houses. Children still babies, none old enough to work in fields by themselves or go to sleep without getting hugs and kisses from mama and daddy. Children healthy and well tended and well loved simply no more, and Eliza's protective circles and protective salves no good at all. Women of Eden gathered around burning houses, holding hands, singing lullabies and spirituals used to put children to bed. Tears like unceasing rain fell, and dark moist earth, wet and soggy, shifted and women fell to their knees, unable or unwilling to stand. Tears carved into the dark earth a small stream that ran clear and meandered through town, stream where grandchildren and great-grandchildren would hunt for slow-moving turtles and well-hidden crayfish.

Men gathered around, lifted women to their feet. Joseph got to her, gave the baby to one of the teenage girls, Sarah, with skin glowing unbearably lovely from the flames.

"You take my baby and put her back to bed. Hear me girl?"

"Yes. I hear you."

Sarah walked away from fire eating up the sky, face wet and voice hoarse, rocking the baby gently and slowly at her hip.

Joseph bent down to Eliza, lifted her up, supported her weight.

"Eliza?"

"Joseph, what about the babies? What about the babies?"

Hate burned up insides like fire burned up houses and personal belongings and dead bodies. Hate so strong no way possible to keep it contained and Eliza scraped and bruised, exhausted from run across town and never-ending tears, powerless. She watched men, her Joseph, run into homes for guns and knives and rakes and shovels, watched women put hysterical children back to bed and send men off with kisses and hugs like men marching into glory, God's kingdom. Eliza too weak to open her mouth, sat still in front of burning homes, face yellow orange red from flames, smell of burning bodies, burning children, in clothes, skin, and hair.

The men were kind to the children, clean shot between the eyes permanently erased terror and shock on small white faces, clean shot between the eyes and ruddy cheeks turned pale, heart-shaped pink lips cold and blue. The women they chased down, held screaming heads in place by ropes and ropes of long blond red dark hair, used rocks to shatter skulls, fingernails to dig out eyes, shovels to break, bend, contort backs. They treated the men like calves and goats hung upside down from trees for slaughter, split bellies, removed heads from neck, watched innards fall, bright red blood, in piles at their feet. They were slow, methodical, didn't hear pleas and screams, didn't hear anything but their women singing songs to dead, burned black children, didn't hear anything but the fire roaring and belching in nighttime sky. Jeremiah Baker, over six feet tall, never sick a day in his life, bloodied his hands first, took pleasure in pain and humiliation because he remembered, was a child during slavery and remembered each fall of the whip, each lash of the cane, each good-bye to a sister or brother or grandmother, good-bye the same as death.

By the time Eliza was on her feet no white people were left alive in all of Eden. She found the men standing over a pile of body parts, hands bloodied, blood smeared across shirts and pants, cheeks and necks and arms, and she was sick, on her knees throwing up her dinner of broiled chicken and baked yams, on her knees in bloody earth, slippery and wet like earth after a nice, long rain. She was stunned by her own failure, her own weakness because body parts piled in the night, white skins glowing beneath belching fire was preventable. She had laid curled into herself while this was being done, laid curled into herself because she knew a huge part of her, huge part that belonged to Eden and loved those black children burning high in nighttime sky, wanted to see this done. Wanted to see bodies piled high and earth dark and wet with revenge.

Eliza rose to her feet, no way to undo what's done, no way to make amends but she had to try, all their lives depended on it. She saw the aftermath of horror on men's faces, the realization that dead white people had friends and family, weren't supposed to die at their black hands.

"We need to bury the bodies."

Jeremiah Baker rubbed blood from his hands onto his blood-soaked shirt.

"I say let them rot right here like the filth they are. Leave them for the foxes and bears."

She stared hard, stared until he backed down.

Joseph stepped in front of her, protecting her even though she knew no protection left anywhere for any of them.

"Act like you got some sense, man. Their death might just mean our death. We need to bury them and we need to do it quick."

They dug all night, the roaring fire eventually burned itself out, nothing left but the shells of houses and slightly glowing debris floating in nighttime sky. They dug in the green surrounding town, pulled up patches and patches of bright green grass and colorful wildflowers, buried all the bodies in a mass grave. They prayed that no one would come looking or asking questions before grass and flowers covered the lonely stretch of bare earth. The men went home, washed the blood from their skin and rakes and hoes and shovels, burned their clothes. They then crawled into bed and cried in the arms of their wives or girlfriends. They weren't murders but they had killed, they weren't bad men but they had sinned, fallen from Eden, no forgiveness for the unforgivable.

Joseph begged her to come home with him.

"It's done, Eliza. Nothing you can do now. Let me take you home. You need to sleep before you fall down."

"Just give me a minute, Joseph. You go on ahead. Please."

Eliza sat alone by the mass grave until afternoon sun high in the sky. Her breasts were aching, full of milk, milk staining her shirt. She cradled her aching breasts and thought of her infant daughter. She measured the cost of the night, knew she'd never see her first daughter grown, nor would her first daughter see her first daughter grown and on down through the generations through the end of time. This was the cost of her powerlessness, the cost of her secret need for vengeance. She knew Jeremiah Baker's family from now until would suffer early deaths, painful deaths, especially the men—the cost of his enjoyment in bloodletting. Too soon to determine the cost for Eden, cost for the land they all loved. She bowed her head and held her arms up to the heavens, sun pleasantly warm, smiling against her flesh.

"Dear Lord, never again. This can never happen again.

No more bloodletting on this land, in Eden. I beg you, dear Lord. No more white people settling here, no more because nothing they touch will grow. Their crops will be infested, their livestock diseased, their gardens meager, their children sickly and ill. They will not be able to thrive in this land, in Eden. They will move, leave us without wanting what we have, without bloodshed on either their part or ours. Dear Lord, this I beg you. By your will and my mama's blood in my veins may this be done."

Eliza felt the power of all the Elizas before her underneath her skin, power of the blood, listened hard and accepted her covenant with God. She looked out over the green of Eden and saw nothing but ashes and salt. She worried over the future—how the people of Eden would ever be able to forgive themselves, or love each other and their children without guilt turning that love vicious and unmanageable. She went home, washed dried blood from her hands and knees, fell into bed, gave thanks for her husband and child, prayed for forgiveness:

> *Have mercy upon me, O God, according to thy loving kindness: according unto the multitudes of thy tender mercies blot out my transgressions.*
> *Wash me thoroughly from mine iniquity, and cleanse me from my sin.*
> *For I acknowledge my transgressions: and my sin is ever before me.*

Chapter Three

In late 1932 the earth of Eden was still soaked scarlet from violence. Eliza knew it as she visited her mama in the graveyard bordering Eden. She was just an infant when the unimaginable happened, when people in the town became mass murders, and her mother helped dig a mass grave in the green surrounding Eden. Her mama told her the story so that she would never forget, just like she would tell the infant daughter sleeping in her womb when the child was old enough to understand. Her husband, Jim, was from Eden. They were married at eighteen and he was a good man, worked down in Cleveland at one the big hotels, and came home each night happy to see her. Jim went to church with her each Sunday and that was beginning and end of his faith. For Eliza and her mother and all the Elizas before and all the Elizas after, faith was the basis of all understanding. She knew that all of Eden was languishing in a kind of purgatory and nothing to do but walk close with God.

Eliza went home from the graveyard, walked through an Eden that was changing, becoming less rural. Many of the adults worked in nearby Cleveland or Lorraine. But there was a bad taste just beneath the illusion of plenty. An entire generation removed from the horror of the sun rising in a night sky, and people in Eden were still fearful of rage buried deep in their guts, hands capable of beating life from the body, stealing air and stopping persistent flow of blood, ashes to ashes and dust to dust. A generation wasn't long enough for the collective memory to fade, to reshape its history so that all things hideous were made bearable.

Eden knew God saw into hearts and heads; saw men corrupt and earth corrupt. They worried about the end, angels with swords racing from the heavens, chopping them down; steady, hard rain for forty days and forty nights and land covered with water; insect plagues destroying crops and gardens, devouring people; firstborn children dead just new from the womb, before even taking a breath.

Eden a different place since the horror of that one night. Eliza believed in souls, knew that pale white bodies buried in the green left some kind of blue-gray haze over the town. Blue-gray haze stayed over Eden all year round, some thought the haze clouds and clouds of small buzzing bugs during the spring and summer, some thought the haze smoke from fireplaces. Years later some would think the haze was pollution rolling in from nearby major cities with skyscrapers and public transportation services. Eliza knew the blue-gray haze nothing more than continuous tears from pale white bodies thrown carelessly in the grave, arms and legs and feet and heads fodder for worms and all manner of creep crawly creatures beneath earth's surface. Sad tears saturated the earth, rose up to the heavens, hung listlessly in the air like snot hung from the noses and mouths of sick, small children.

Men avoided each other, stayed close to homes and hearth, unable to wash blood from their hands, get rid of scent of blood riding their skin like in early fall good smell of natural rot heavy in the air and always in hair and clothes. Women opened arms, offered forgiveness for acts they had no right to forgive. The women tried to become saints, failed miserably, became nothing more than nags and dirty hands always scratching at open, oozing wounds. Eden no longer the same as biblical Eden, no longer piece of Heaven on Earth with lush green standing guard like angels wielding swords. Eden was no naked and childlike safe place in the world for a victimized people. The town of Eden, before dead bodies buried in mass grave, a people who pictured themselves largely without sin. They didn't learn until far too late that their shiny, untarnished picture of themselves the greatest sin of all. There were serpents in the garden, serpents in the fields, serpents living happy and content beneath beds and in dark corners of well-tended homes.

They didn't talk about the mass grave in Eden, didn't talk about pale white-skinned bodies rotting and nourishing the earth. Tried to ignore bright colorful wild flowers growing tall and lush and thick over mass grave, so sturdy and strong they were almost impossible to cut down. Tried to ignore guilt and shame eating at bone and raw flesh of insides, festering in homes, causing all manner of chaos and discord.

Husbands and wives argued because beds not made just right, chicken and steak not cooked well, floors and tables dirty, always attracting dust. Brothers and sisters fought over dolls and toys and sticks and rocks. Just about every baby in Eden disgruntled and evil and miserable from colic, weak screams desperate and long and continuous. Crops no longer as abundant, farm animals weak and sickly, little meat on the bone, houses sunk in the earth, foundations rotting. They knew—every man woman and child—there was a long, slow fall for Eden coming. Long slow fall that would last for generations and generations, no one exempt, no one excused.

They remembered prayer. Every night and every morning on hands and knees giving thanks and begging for some kind of peace, some kind of way to deal with what they had done, the stranger people they had become as a result. Before pale, white-skinned bodies buried in mass grave easy for them to be good, to wander Eden with light and laughter in the heart and eyes. Eden before the mass grave was a land of plenty and no want; land of safety and no shame; land of abundance and no greed, no desperate fear that what was theirs always in danger of being stolen.

White people with red golden dark flowing hair came looking for brothers and sisters and cousins nieces and nephews and cousins. They came looking, were startled by uncompromising beauty of the land, grass green and wet, trees healthy and sturdy shooting up past sky all the way to God's Heaven.

Eden perfected lies, told stories about white people staying in Eden for brief moments, setting up house, growing gardens, raising livestock and packing it all up and heading west. Easy lies because most people headed west for endless sunshine and land. Most people easily fell prey to the American disease that life was always better somewhere else.

Some white people tried to stay, accepted lies, built homes and shipped furniture for living rooms and bedrooms, livestock for newly built barns and chicken coops, some grew gardens. They worked the land diligently, white people used to hands plowing at rich, dark earth, hands turning and turning moist soil, soil so healthy and rich that they waited on abundant crops, plump and fat livestock, never considered the possibility of failure. Never considered how long and cold the winters were when no meat in the icehouse, when cows refused to let down milk, when grain refused to grow in the spring and summer. Everything they touched turned to salt, ruined. They left the same way they assumed sisters and brothers and nephews and nieces and cousins left, wagons loaded full so that they dipped and dragged in the center, wagons headed west, over the horizon to someplace, somewhere better.

Eliza tended to Eden the way her mama tended to Eden. Tended it more carefully because people in Eden lived with wet in the corner of their eyes. The wet hit dark moist earth and stole some of the earth's sweetness, some of the earth's ability to grow anything with little, if any help. Wet mingled in the feed that they gave to chickens, the hay they gave to horses and cows, animals chewed and swallowed sadness, became thin and weak, sadness carved animal flesh from the inside out. Wet served with dinner each and every night, extra seasoning, salt and pepper, confused the flavor of food. Chicken tasted like greens and greens tasted like tripe and tripe tasted like beans and beans tasted like pie. Children ate because they had to, not because it was good, even the cookies, cakes, and pies.

Eliza made herbal tinctures for families, something to help food go down better, entire households silent over dinner because bad food, confused taste buds robbed all the joy and laughter from a meal, dinner nothing more than another chore. She mixed special herbs in chicken feed, in hay used for horses and cows. Sometimes it worked, sometimes it didn't, hard to keep any living thing healthy with blue-gray haze overhead and fresh salty tears embedded deep in the soil.

Jim brought a new car early in 1940, a shiny black Ford in the fall, the first car she'd ever been in. She was charmed with its wonderful, clean exterior, no smell of any kind of animal anywhere. Eliza watched him drive the car down the road to their house for the first time, her daughter on her side, her daughter's long legs hanging well passed her hips. She knew, as soon as he pulled the car up on the dirt road leading to their home that her teas and salves and herbs and prayers would do absolutely no good, she was staring down her own death, the shiny black Ford coming slow and insistent for her.

Chapter Four

Aspasia and her mama, the great granddaughter of the first Eliza, sat on sandy beaches of Lake Erie. Aspasia was only six years old when they started going to beaches during the weekends. Aspasia dimly understood that Mama was running out of time, needed to talk to her about the past before the words were all gone. Aspasia didn't have the same relationship that her older sister, Eliza, had with Mama. Aspasia wasn't firstborn; there were parts of Mama that were quite simply unavailable to her. They went late in the afternoon, right before the sun was about to set. Mama spread blankets out on the damp sand. Aspasia sat between Mama's legs, Mama's arms holding her. Mama played in Aspasia's hair as she talked.

"I was born in 1933, the only child of really good parents. People always talk about only children being lonely, but I had Mama and she was enough. My earliest memories are of my mama's kitchen. The brilliance of the white tiles, the scent of pine that always lingered, the way the sunlight streamed in through the windows, through the bright yellow lace curtains to land on my face. I had Mama's name the same way Eliza has my name, all of us continuations of the same people, all of us with mystery and magic just beneath the skin. I remember my bedroom with its whitewashed walls and hardwood floors that held a shine so bright that they could blind you. Daddy smelled like the woods and cold November days. He'd come in from work and pick me up and hold me for a long time. Mama had the sweetest voice imaginable, and soft hands, and her skin always smelled of lavender and potpourri.

"I remember trees. There were always trees in Eden bending over gardens and pavements and parks. In the summer providing shade, in the fall bright, colorful leaves scattering all over the place. I can see Mama cooking at the stove, preparing to step out with Daddy on a Saturday night. There was the Apple Festival in the center of town, the smell and taste of sausages and pastries. There was church on Sundays, the preacher sweating and laboring—a slave to the Holy Ghost. All the ladies dressed in their Sunday best, drenched in perfume, hats tilted arrogantly to the side. The men all in their Sunday suits, long legs crossed elegantly at the knee, shoes polished and dressed socks starched.

"As a child I caught lightning bugs in the backyard on cool summer evenings. I placed them, with care, into a glass jar so that they could glow only for me. I went on a lot of trips across town to visit my granddaddy, Poppop, for the weekends. I sat on his lap on Saturdays in the early afternoon, protected from the sun by the shade of the porch while he ran his hands over my arms or through the rough thickness of my hair. He told me stories, or made me laugh with his teasing and nonsense. There was so much pleasure in his soft wrinkled hands against my face, smoothing my eyebrows, gliding across my forehead. I loved the white hair of his head—I'd constantly play in it, shaping, combing, messing up again.

"I remember the morning Mama and Daddy failed to fetch me from Poppop's. We waited all day and all night for them to come, only to be told the next morning by a police officer standing under the shade of the porch that they had died in a car accident. A car accident and Mama hardly ever rode in Daddy's car. Mama didn't even know how to drive, that's how scared of cars she was. And I guess she was right to be scared because a car eventually killed her.

"I was nine years old that year and I still remember how quiet Poppop's house seemed that day, like it was holding its breath. Poppop was quiet, too. Whenever his gaze chanced to rest on me he looked right through me.

"The morning of the funeral all Poppop's and Mama and Daddy's friends gathered at the house; all of them were hugging and kissing me calling me 'that poor child . . .' in hushed tones. I was just a little girl, all bones and hair and eyes. I was confused and no one would talk to me or explain. I crept through Poppop's house, now my home during those days before the funeral, so silent, like I wasn't there at all. I stayed hidden in my room, playing with dolls, holding conversations with my dead parents, not understanding death because no one had bothered to explain it to me.

"Then there was the funeral. I clutched Poppop's hand as we walked down that unending aisle leading to the very first pew and the closed mahogany caskets that were so close that I could reach out and touch them. I listened, bug eyed, to the preacher's sermon. I fell asleep when the choir began singing 'Amazing Grace.' Still holding Poppop's hand. They buried Mama and Daddy the next day, buried them in earth green and ripe with springtime and blue skies overhead. It wasn't until I saw them place the coffins in the ground that I knew Mama and Daddy weren't coming back and realized that death meant not seeing, or hearing, or touching a person again.

"After the funeral there was an eternity of silence in the house that we lived, a silence that was calm in its stillness, a silence that even nature didn't bother to disturb. We buried ourselves beneath the silence, created a world of suspended sound. Only we existed and floated upon the air. Even the music drifting from Poppop's phonograph—Bessie and Billie wailing blues—didn't have the power to break the silence. The opened windows refused to admit sound; the din of crickets and the song of birds was transformed into tiny ice crystals as it tried to enter through the window so that I—if I were still enough—could actually watch as the sounds fell to the earth like raindrops or snow. There was no conversation, just gestures and mouths shaping words that couldn't be heard. Things got so bad that people stopped visiting. The house gathered dust and a stale smell as doors and windows were open less often and the shades were always down to keep out sunlight.

"The silence in no time at all rid me of my laughter, cured me of my tears, and stole my youth. I was an old woman—with sagging breasts and twisted limbs—in a child's body. The silence was with me everywhere I went, to school, on the way to the store for Poppop, when I explored the backyards of neighbors. I saw people and waved and smiled, but I never heard anyone. I only heard my own voice, and with it I'd hold endless conversations. I wasn't lonely. Poppop and I would pass each other in the silence of the house and move on; on to another room, another corner. We were like ghosts who, day and night, wandered and haunted our own home.

"The blood shocked me from the silence. At first I had no idea of its origins, my mind was an absolute blank on which no awareness or knowledge had been written. And the blood escaped in rivulets that, as the day wore on, grew into great rivers that churned and crashed and finally found shelter at the gentle slope of my thighs. There it hardened as I tried to overcome my complete bewilderment. My body became to me a great horrifying mystery that I couldn't ever hope to solve; my body was in no way a part of me. How could it be when it had produced this, which I knew nothing of? Rising from the depths of my confusion came the horrible thought that I was dying. I was scared. Each night I crawled into bed, alone in the silence, a dishrag shoved between my thighs to catch and, if God were merciful, halt the fatal flow of blood. Poppop never realized what I was going through. I couldn't find the words to tell him, and he wouldn't have heard me through the silence.

"Miracle of miracles I awoke on the seventh day to find the dishrag between my thighs white, free of any blood. I lay stunned and disbelieving at first—I had no idea what this meant. The bleeding, for all I knew, could begin again. So I got up and went about my Saturday chores, every hour or so suspiciously checking my underpants. But a week passed and there was no bleeding. I opened my eyes and it was as if I had been blind my entire life; the world was new again, and there was so much to discover. I was stunned by the abundance of sky overhead and grass underfoot. The sun shining in my eyes, or on any part of my body totally dazzled me. The rain falling gently in the form of a drizzle or fiercely in the form of a thunderstorm had the power to move me to awe and tears. I would rush outside to feel rain on my face and the wet earth between my toes. There was the beauty of Lake Erie at sunset, or on a foggy day. But I liked the rain the most; in the rain there was a sorrowful beauty that reminded me of Poppop's blues.

"Gradually, the wall of silence crumbled around me. I could hear again! I listened intently to all sounds, from the sigh and groan of automobiles, to the wheezing of Poppop's snores, to the roar and song of the wind.

"A month later, surprising me, the blood came once again, flowing like a river from between my schoolgirl thighs. I was annoyed, but I didn't fear for my life; I shoved a dishrag between my legs and suffered through it. It wasn't until the following year that I learned, in the bathroom at school from a girlfriend, that the spilling of my blood each month was completely natural. I was shocked. It seemed utterly unnatural to me. I was fourteen years old that year. My body was changing form and shape; I gained a roundness of hip and breast, my waist acquired a subtle curve that forced my whole figure into prominence. At school boys began to notice me and follow me through the halls as if I held all the secrets in the universe at the joining of my thighs. I was beautiful.

"At home, Poppop continued to dwell in his world of silence. He would lie in his bed or rock in his rocking chair. He never spoke to me, would simply nod his head in my general direction to convey all of his thoughts and feelings. I understood that I was on my own, and set about raising myself and taking care of Poppop.

"People started coming to me around that time. Mostly women. They wanted a little something to bring down a high fever in a child, to fend off hysteria in a sister or close friend. Seems like everybody in Eden looked to me to make their lives a little better, to take some of the sting out of living. I didn't mind. I had people to talk to after all those years alone. I had family. I remembered everything Mama had ever told me since birth, seems like I was groomed to take Mama's place. I was mature enough at that age to realize that it's blood that makes you who you are, that blood makes it impossible to be anything else. What I didn't know I learned from older women in the community. Ms. Betsy taught me all about herbs. Ms. Annie Queen taught me how to talk to the Christ child high in Heaven. Ms. Audrey taught me how to hold back the rains and quiet the thunder with just the whisper of my voice. All those women nurtured the power already in me, watched me become more than what I was, watched me become more my mother and all the mothers before me.

"High school kind of passed in this boring blur, nothing at all to tell. Just more silence at home, and silliness in school. I was never a teenager. I went away to school when I was eighteen, but I always knew I was coming back to Eden, had no choice but to come back. I went down South to Bennett College. At that time most blacks went to black schools. And Bennett was lovely, an all woman's college. It was lush and green and welcoming. But above all it was peaceful and safe. I stayed there for two years until I had to come home when Poppop had his first heart attack.

"It seems like as soon as I got there I started seeing William, your daddy. He was cute, and sweet, and funny. Just all the time making me laugh and smile. I thought he was wonderful, just a really fine man. We had become lovers on our fourth date, but it felt like we had always been lovers. I didn't want to leave him when Poppop got sick, even though he was starting to squeeze all the air out of me. Relationships are funny like that. They start off good, and before you know it things turn bad and you can't figure out why. Your daddy just started asking for so much of me. And I was really just a girl, no life experience at all.

"I thought that we could make something between us work, and make it good. The night I told him I was leaving he proposed. Can you imagine? Just proposed and said that he was willing to come home with me, willing to fit his life around mine. Do you know what I remember most about that night? His arm around me. It was so heavy, and I knew, no matter how much effort I put into it, I'd never be able to remove it. But I was twenty, and I had to go home to that house and silence to take care of a dying man. I didn't want to do it alone. So I said yes.

"As soon as I said yes William began to make me tired. Just always badgering me. We went home to Eden and Poppop. William wanted me to spend all my time on him. He was jealous of Poppop, jealous of girlfriends, and even jealous of you and Eliza. He was jealous of all of Eden because I was a part of Eden in a way that excluded him completely. It felt like he was trying to take everything from me. Everything. I wasn't going to let him do that to me, wasn't going to let him put me in a tiny box for his use. And so I fought him.

"I had Eliza when I was twenty-three. Poppop died the year before and I was sad all during the pregnancy, wishing he could have seen my first child. And, my God, that girl's birth was painful. I think it hurt so bad because it was so much of a shock. I just wasn't prepared for it. And then you came; your birth was almost painless. The doctor placed you in my arms and I stared at your red face for the very first time. You were so solemn; there were no shrieks and cries of protest. Eliza had put on a show when the doctor first let me hold her.

"Don't do what I did; don't give yourself away to the first person that comes along. Most people don't ever really live. One of the best and most used excuses is love. When I met William all he wanted to do was take care of me. No one, not since my parents died, had ever wanted to take care of me, to make sure I was happy. I was used to taking care of Eden, went to bed most nights worrying about the entire town. I thought it would be so nice to give myself up to someone who wanted to look after me—I didn't realize how hard it would be to get myself back.

"I brought it on myself. I can't blame William. He wanted me, and I gave myself away, and then he wouldn't let me breathe. I know he's your daddy, but you can't imagine what our marriage has been like—always fighting to get me back. You know the worst mistake I made? I loved indiscriminately. When I first met William he was nice and sweet, and he cared for me. I think that I started to love him, or at least told him that I did because he wanted me to. And I think—this sounds horrible—but I think I was bored. There was nothing better to do than love him, so why not? I gave myself away . . . And now I'm all out of time.

"And we're still arguing about who hurt who the most, even though there's no more time. Don't believe those fairy-tales about the beautiful princess rescued by some hand-some prince. Love's not always like that. Love, in all its variations, is not invulnerable, not a thing meant to last for-ever. Love can hurt you. Look at me; I'm dying of it.

"My whole life has been Eden and my family. I know the nickname of every child in Eden, know the monthly cycles of every woman, and know the inadequacies of every man. Sometimes there are no choices. Some things are just meant to be and nothing anyone can do to change it. Eden like a yoke around many a day, like a baby I have to constantly look after. And not even a sweet-tempered baby. No, Eden is a baby comfortable with throwing temper tantrums and destroying anything and everything it doesn't like. I know Eden like I know you and Eliza, like the back of my hand. Sometimes we do what has to be done because no one else will and that's fine, too."

Chapter Five

William came to Eden because of love, because a woman with deep red skin and big brown eyes smiled at him. The sweetness of her smile made him want, made him ache, and he had thought that all he needed in life was her, his Eliza. He moved to Eden for her. He tried to ignore the blue-gray haze in the skies. He tried to ignore the intimate, vacant eyes of the residents. He tried to ignore the sickly sweet smell of blood and guts and innards. William couldn't get over or figure out that smell. He was raised on farm, knew how the scent of butchered animals lingered on the air for days. But by the time he arrived in Eden in the winter of 1956 there were no farms left in Eden, there were no animals except for a few hens that some old women kept for eggs.

William didn't like Eden, thought a million times about moving his family, his wife and two daughters, back to North Carolina. He knew his wife wouldn't go, wouldn't leave a place that she carried lovingly and carefully on her small back.

William sat on the porch of his house and watched his

children play. Aspasia was still a child, and Eliza was tentatively wandering the long road toward womanhood. He wanted to pick Eliza up and run far and fast. He knew the life that waited for her, knew the sacrifices that would be demanded of her. Sometimes William thought about the future that awaited his child and wanted to burn the whole town down, to dance with his girls around the smoke and ashes.

It wasn't until he met his wife that he began to believe in fate, in God, in something. It wasn't until she smiled at him that first time that he began to consider that maybe there were things that were unavoidable, burdens that had to be born, sins that had to be committed. He knew now that he would have ended up the same place, in Eden, no matter what he did or didn't do.

William first arrived in Eden during the winter, and winters in Eden forever more astounded him. In North Carolina winter never actually came. It teased and threatened and some days you felt its bite and it hurt. But winter never came. In January the temperature was still mild and the grass, for the most part, was still green and the trees had most of their leaves. Nothing hibernated.

The summers were hell. Heat like you wouldn't believe, and no place to go, no way to get away from it. The heat followed people into their houses, hunted them down at night in their beds. It forced people into a stupor—getting up and walking from one place to another stole all their energy. Crossing the road to visit neighbors was difficult; traveling a ways to the next town was damn near impossible even if you did have a car. There were mosquitoes. They gorged on the blood of unsuspecting victims until they fell to the grass or porch dead. If you were to kill one between the two palms of your hands they'd leave a bright crimson mark. Small children stared, amazed that crimson mark just might be their blood.

William Todd grew up in Bear Creek, North Carolina. A country place at a time when most places in North Carolina were either country or small towns. He climbed trees and helped his daddy on the farm and watched his mama cook and waited on Sunday dinners because Sunday dinners were the best of the week.

His mama served collards and ham and cornbread, and he really didn't care if he had to go to church in the mornings first. He went to a segregated school, which was fine by him—he didn't desire to go to school with white folks.

He loved the South. His father taught him to treasure the land, his mother taught him to appreciate the customs, and he convinced himself that he was living a right fine life. There was always food on the table, maybe not enough to keep his belly full or exactly what he wanted, but he never went hungry. He liked school, and was a good student.

His mama was proud of him. When her friends came over the house to visit she always bragged on him.

"My baby's going to be a doctor or something. You just wait, my baby he going to be something."

His father took him and his brothers out to the fields. His eyes were clear and his back was straight from years of working.

His father never wanted him to leave the land.

"All this, all this is ours. Ours. Put your hand on the dirt. Can you feel it? Ain't no dirt in the world like North Carolina dirt. Take care of it and it will take care of you always."

It broke his father's heart to see all the blacks leaving the South for the North. The South was beautiful, too beautiful a land to just up and leave.

William promised his father.

"Daddy, I'll never leave. I'll take care of our land."

His father smiled at him and William could see the relief on his face.

There was college, and he went to North Carolina A&T State University in Greensboro, North Carolina to study agriculture. It was a whole new world. There were the white people. He felt that he were somehow better than them—neither he or any of his race, as far as he could tell, practiced intentional cruelty. He really felt no need to be around them, but realized that whether or not he wanted to go to school with them, or live side-by-side with them, should be his choice.

He helped organize the first student sit-ins in Greensboro. They all marched down to the Woolworth in the center of town, books in hand. It wasn't a far walk, no distance at all, but he felt as if it were the farthest he ever had to walk in his life. He smelled his own funk and his own fear. He went in and sat and prayed that he would have the power not to kill. The white folks prodded and poked and insulted and dragged them out of the store. He kept thinking, Lord, don't let me kill one of these crackers, please.

William knew that if he went back and had to go through that again he would kill. Killing, anyhow, made more sense than begging and groveling and letting those people spit on him—kill them all and the problem would be solved.

Just a ways from A&T, a hop, skip and a jump really, was Bennett College, a school for black women. These were ladies.

If they were seen off-campus they had on skirts, pretty blouses, and stylish shoes, and walked with their heads high as if all that were common and coarse was beneath them. Well, he was common and coarse. He didn't mean to be, but that was the truth and there it was. He was good country folk and he wasn't going to change for no uppity colored girl.

Then he saw Eliza Jones walking about the community with a little package in her hands. He knew right away that she was a Bennett Belle because she had on stylish slacks, a cotton blouse, and a leather purse strapped to her shoulder. She was the most beautiful thing that he had ever seen. She wasn't high yellow, she wasn't dark or even brown—she was red, the prettiest, darkest, deepest red that he ever saw. The redness of her skin moved him. He stared, wanting to taste, to touch, to hold, just watch forever.

He walked over to her all calm and gentlemen like.

"Do you need help with that package?"

She turned to him like she was surprised, but really this was just a bit of feminine guile on her part.

She had noticed him noticing her.

"No, thank you. I just have to deliver this food to Mrs. Johnson."

She was all sugar and sweetness, but cunning also, waiting.

She asked, "Do you know Mrs. Johnson?"

"No, no I don't."

William hesitantly falling into step beside her, terrified that she would tell him to go away.

"Well, she helps feed the children down at the church at the corner of Market Street." Eliza said, and smiled.

That smile got all up inside of William.

"I've been by there once or twice."

There was a silence that was pleasant and William didn't remove his eyes from her face. She had the most beautiful face, all big eyes and full lips and soft, butter soft, skin.

They came to a stop. It was the middle of September, and the day was hot, still.

"What's your name?"

William moved closer to her so that he actually smelled her.

"Eliza Queen Jones."

She was breathless, whether from the heat or his nearness he didn't know.

"That's a pretty name."

She blushed, turning that red skin a deeper shade along her cheekbones.

"Thank you. And your name is? . . ."

She waited, and again he took a step closer to her, she quickly retreated, but not that far.

"William Marcus Todd."

He smiled, and the smile implied that he was going to know her, whether she liked it or not, this was what he was going to do and she'd better just accept it.

They started walking again in silence, a silence that burned. Eliza bit her lower lip in nervousness. William watched her. They reached the church and William didn't want her to leave.

Their steps slowed, and they shuffled unwillingly along. Finally, there was no help for it and they were standing directly in front of the double doors.

"Well, William . . ."

"Thank you for letting me walk you here. I enjoyed myself."

"You're welcome, it was nice talking to you."

"Eliza, do you think that maybe, sometimes, if it isn't too much trouble . . ."

"Yes?"

"Could I maybe come see you sometimes?"

Eliza bit her lip uncertainly, and he held his breath as she gave him a measuring glance that encompassed all of him, from his head to his toes.

"Well, all right then."

"When would be a good time for you?"

"Saturday afternoon, is that good for you?"

"Oh, yes. Saturday is real good for me. I'll see you then?"

"Yes. All right."

"I'll be seeing you, Eliza. I'll be seeing you."

It wasn't until after she had disappeared into the church that he realized that she had a Northern accent. Her voice was soft on the ears.

That Saturday he called upon her and they sat and talked in the parlor of her dorm. He discovered that she was from Ohio, that her parents died when she was young, and her grandfather raised her.

They went for walks in the parks and he took her to playgrounds where he, as if she were a child, pushed her on the swings. She flew high up, her shirts twirling about her, her laughter resounding in the air. Their first argument came when he killed a bee. Killing a bee was a casual thing to him, he didn't even have to think about it. He saw the yellow jack buzzing around his head and quickly squashed it between his palms. She was in the middle of a sentence.

Her voice faltered, and then stopped altogether. She looked at him with sad, wondering eyes.

"You didn't have to kill it."

"Kill what?"

William was at a total loss.

"That bee. It wasn't bothering you, not really."

William, unable to help himself, laughed.

"Girl, hush. It was only a bee. Nobody's going to miss it."

"But that's not the point. You killed it for no reason."

She was really upset.

"So I'm a bee killer, right? What's going to happen to me now, do I go to jail or what?"

William teased, pulling her into his arms.

Eliza stiffened and moved away from him.

"It's not funny, William."

He was amazed by her sensitivity.

"I can't believe this is really bothering you."

"I got to get back. I got studying to do."

"You ready to go because of that damn bee?"

"You didn't have to kill it."

"Well, let me take you back then, and I hope I don't accidentally kill anything else."

He was furious.

They argued a lot. She was like no one else. Her thoughts were constantly shifting and changing. He was fascinated and he fell in love. It got to the point where he knew, just knew that he couldn't live without her. He spent all of his free time with her, sulked if she said that she had something else to do.

She wasn't allowed to have men in her dorm room, so on the weekends he took her to his fraternity house so they could make love. They made love on the bed, or the roughness of the carpet.

Eliza kept up a continuous chant.

"Oh, William. Oh, William. Good Lord."

He bent her over tables and pushed into her from behind. He sat down on chairs and made her ride him. She let him do anything he wanted with her. She was like falling, and he fell, couldn't get enough.

Her grandfather had a stroke, and all of a sudden life changed. They were coming back from the movies, and they sat in his old, battered Ford. It was late January, the spring semester just started.

"William, I'm leaving school."

Her eyes were already focused down the road, her thoughts already headed toward Ohio.

"When you coming back?"

He wrapped himself around her.

She shook her head.

"I'm not coming back."

William pulled away from her, turned her so that she faced him directly.

"But why?"

He sputtered, shocked.

"My grandfather had a stroke. He's in the hospital. They called me this morning. I have to leave. I'm all that he's got."

William stared at her, her features were blurred within the darkness of the car, but he could make out her large, brown eyes. She was staring right through him. He wondered what she was thinking, what she was really thinking. She would never tell him, her thoughts were exactly that—hers. He wished that she wasn't so reserved, but it was her remoteness that attracted him to her, that fascinated him more than sweet smiles and shy vulnerability ever could.

She was stubborn and unbending, fiercely independent and startling direct. More than anything he wanted her to belong to him, to love him. She was leaving for good, he was never going to see or touch her again. The thought of that was unbearable. He couldn't let that happen.

"Can't you just go home and make sure he's okay, and then come back to school?"

"No, I want to go home. He needs me, William. All of Eden, Ohio, needs me, and I'm tired of fighting it. I'm really tired."

She turned her face away from him, and he felt that to her it was all settled.

"Are you sick of me, Eliza? You sick of me, too?"

He waited patiently for her to answer him, not knowing

what he'd do if she told him that she didn't want him anymore.

"William, this really isn't about you. I don't think I could ever really get tired of you, anyway. It's just that I have to go home. You don't understand because you live here, it's easy for you to get home if something happens. If I stayed here I'd always be worrying about him, I'd always be worrying about every man, woman, and child in that town. You have no idea what I am to Eden, what Eden is to me. I can't do it."

William sat perfectly still, hands gripping the steering wheel, considering the situation from all angles. What was he to do? He could cry. He could shout and holler and scream at her, try to force her to see reason—reason being nothing more than his point of view.

He would go home with her. It made perfect sense to him, because really it made no sense at all. To leave everything—his family, his home, all that made up his life—for her. The idea was insane, but there was nothing left for him to do.

He turned toward her, studying the elegance of her profile. He wished that there was a little more light so that he could see the deep red of her skin. He was nervous. Did he really want this, want her so very much?

He took a deep breath, let it out on a long sigh. "Eliza, do you want to marry me?"

She stared at him for the longest time, as if his words carried no sound and had no meaning.

"William, I'm going home."

She said as if that were answer enough.

"I know you're going home. You already told me that. What I asked you is, do you want to marry me?"

She spread her hands in a helpless gesture.

"Marry you and stay here?"

"Marry me, and I'll go home with you."

"Just like that?"

"Yeah, I guess so."

"All right. Yes, I'll marry you."

Two days after the ceremony the Greyhound bus stopped at the bus station in Eden, Ohio. The beginning of February and snow was on the ground. William and Eliza left the warmth of the bus. They were attacked by frigid air and brisk winds. William had never been so cold in his life. He picked up their bags and followed Eliza into the bus station. Eliza called a cab. They waited in the station, watching snowflakes fall for over an hour.

The cab finally arrived, bright yellow clashing violently with the dreariness of the day. Eliza didn't pay any attention to the town as the cab crept through it—it was home for her and unremarkable. William was fascinated by the spaciousness of the place. It was small, but seemed huge, its borders endless. It was early afternoon and he saw children trekking home, footprints following behind them. He was surprised that they actually had to go to school in such weather—there was at least six inches of snow on the ground. In North Carolina, even the hint of snow was enough for all schools to close. If there was snow on the ground everything came to a complete stop—people didn't leave their houses, markets and stores were closed, and roads were shut down.

They reached the house. The driver helped William unload the suitcases. William paid him and he left. Suddenly it was just he and Eliza standing in the cold, husband and wife coming home. The house was large and rundown. Eliza fumbled for her door key. He was cold; he stood there on the porch with bags at his feet. She finally managed to open the door. For a moment he was dazed by warmth and didn't see anything.

The furniture was old and heavy, sturdy furniture. There were dull, hardwood floors that would have been beautiful if polished to a shine. The walls were covered in deep rose wallpaper that was faded and stained in places. It needed to be taken down. William was very careful about how he touched things, some of the chairs didn't look like they could bear his weight. He realized how out of place he was in this house, his home. Eliza walked around, touching things. He never saw her so comfortable.

"Do you want me to take these bags upstairs?"

He asked, standing awkwardly in front of the door, feeling large and clumsy.

"In a minute. Come here, I want to show you something."

He practically tiptoed over to where she was standing beside the mantelpiece.

"This is my mother, Eliza."

She pointed to a picture. Both mother and daughter had the same deep red skin, same large brown eyes, high foreheads, and full mouths.

"You look just like her. You all have the same name?"

"Yes, it's the same with all firstborn girls in my family. This is my daddy."

He was light skinned, almost yellow, his features sharp and strong. "You look nothing like him. Wait a minute, you telling me we're going to have to name our daughter Eliza, too."

"Yes, firstborn daughters are always Eliza. Most people say I look at least a little like Daddy."

"Okay, I guess I can live with that. Two Elizas running around the house acting crazy."

She laughed.

"See, you know you not right. This is my grandfather."

Her grandfather had the same red skin.

"This is your mama's daddy?"

"Yeah, you can tell?"

"All of you got that skin."

This little old red man was the real reason he was in Ohio and married.

"Will your grandfather mind that I'm here, that you married me?"

Her grandfather was in the hospital recovering from a stroke, and he had married his only grandchild and moved into his house. He didn't feel right about it.

Eliza laughed it off.

"No, Poppop won't mind a bit."

William wasn't as sure.

"What should I call him?"

She shrugged. "Call him Gene. Eugene's his first name, and all his friends call him Gene."

William didn't know what being married to Eliza meant at first, didn't realize until anyone and everyone knocked at their door all times of the day and night for tea for sick babies and poultices for aching bones and tinctures for colds and coughs and fevers. They knocked at their door for prayer and comfort and magic and things all better. William always fought Eliza for attention. He loved her and was just a little scared of who she was, who everyone in Eden thought she was. William was always frustrated and angry. He realized that love was the same as hate in Eden. Blue-gray haze in the air made it easy to be cruel one moment and repentant the next, he was always twisted inside out and outside in until the day he died dreaming of his daddy's land in North Carolina.

Chapter Six

Eden was overcome, seduced by love during the 1960s. Strong love like winter past and rain over, singing of birds a heavy melody in the air. Trees and flowers bloomed and blossomed, gave a good smell. Love drifted from green surrounding Eden like pillars of smoke, perfumed with pollen from flowers and fresh grass, all the powders of nature. Everyone in Eden compelled to search for their beloved; they roamed the streets of Eden, dazed, hungry for love. They sought love with greedy hands and open bleeding mouths, found nothing. They went down into gardens and green to eat listlessly of fruits and vegetables, chew on grass like sick cats or dogs.

Eden was under a spell, no waters enough to appease thirst for love, no food enough to ease appetite for love, no money enough to buy love. Eden knew during that long decade when the entire country, the entire world suddenly and irreversibly changed, that love was as strong as death, jealousy as cruel as the grave.

The ground for the Sweet Cake factory was turned over in the fall of 1964. Eden heard the hum of machines from the highway; saw machines lined up along the highway to Cleveland, waited on new jobs. Everyone in Eden used to the hour-long commute to Cleveland to work in major hotels, restaurants, bookstores, and clothing and hardware outlets. Working men and women tired of the long drive to Cleveland watched impatiently as the factory rose like magic from flat green grass. Mamas at home taking care of babies and gardens and dinner and breakfast and lunch heard the hum from the highway as a breathless high note singing possibilities.

The Sweet Cake factory was finished by spring, large modern, glass structure in the middle of flat green grass. The factory was imposing, dark mirrored walls reflecting sun and clouds and cars parked in the acres and acres of car lots. From the outside in no way at all to tell that cakes, pies, cookies, donuts made in vast amounts, shipped all across the state of Ohio and a few neighboring states as well. Sweet Cakes quickly became an Ohio specialty despite random complaints year after year that the cakes and pies and cookies didn't taste the same, didn't rest heavy and sticky sweet on the tongue, not enough sugar, butter, milk.

The factory threw open its doors the spring of 1965. Half the adults in Eden applied and received jobs on the assembly line, astonished that cakes and donuts and pies treated like parts for cars and radios and televisions, all made on never-ceasing-unless-something-wrong assembly lines. The Sweet Cake factory offered decent pay and health benefits and it was close, no more than a half hour from Eden. Men and women used to getting up at five in the morning to make the drive to Cleveland didn't get out of bed until at least six, stayed under covers, enjoyed leisurely breakfast, eased instead of rushed to work. Women had enough time to get children fed and dressed for school without resorting to threats and hysterics.

It wasn't until the following fall when colored leaves scattered across ground like plush, expensive carpet that the smell of butter and sugar from the Sweet Cake factory took over Eden. The town was in the grip of a yellow butter haze, air smelled like sugar water. Smell strong and always there, no escape by closing windows or turning on fans. Smell so strong and so sweet that old women refused to bake and young children stopped racing to the convenience store to buy prettily packaged mounds of sugar, always felt as if they had a tummy ache coming on. Sweet Cakes piled on the store aisles, fell like garbage to clean, well-swept floors. At first, only the men in Eden enjoyed butter and sugar constantly in the air, walked around with eyes closed slowly chewing as if what they had far too good to share.

Eliza, great granddaughter of Eliza who led slaves from the wilderness and grand daughter of Eliza who piled bodies high in mass grave, waited for something to happen. She waited as soon as breathing butter and sugar the same as breathing air in Eden. No way for all that sweetness to be coated to lungs and throats and the insides of noses without having some kind of affect. She waited, played with her two little girls, Eliza and Aspasia, cooked dinner and fought and slept with her husband, William, and waited some more. She wasn't sure what she was waiting on, and maybe no reason at all to be alarmed, but each morning she woke up to yellow butter haze in the sky a sinking in her stomach, a break in her breath.

Women started coming to her first, women who worked down at the Sweet Cake factory. They couldn't get the smell of butter and sugar out of their clothes and hair and skin no matter how often they washed, how often they sat in scalding hot water with eyes closed to avoid layers and layers of upward floating steam. Eliza didn't notice her own smell was the same as butter and sugar until other women started coming to her. It wasn't until other women complained that she realized butter and sugar in the air day and night a permanent part of her DNA, no way to get rid of the smell. She knew that if there was no way to get the smell off her own body no way at all for her to help others and certainly no way to make butter sugar yellow haze altogether vanish from the sky.

Eliza gave women herbal soaks and soaps for the bath, herbal creams to slather on skin morning and night, perfumes made from essential oils, herbal teas to clean out insides, leave them good and fresh. Nothing worked. Women still smelled like butter and sugar, sugar haze still in the sky, men still chewed slow like they had something far too good to share.

Eliza waited because she knew women didn't go around smelling like butter and sugar, with butter and sugar all mixed up and confused in DNA without some kind of something happening. She was bringing her girls home from the park, her oldest daughter, Eliza, holding tight to Aspasia's child-fat hand, when she noticed her girlfriend, Pat, turning chocolate candy wrapper inside out to lick at chocolate smashed and smeared against plastic. Pat was thin, didn't eat too much of anything, and licking and sucking at the candy wrapper like all the goodness in the world there for her to find. Men on corners and sitting at stoops sucked hard at lollipops, the usual cigarettes gone, tongues and teeth and lips bright red from cherry and watermelon lollipops. Children playing in front and backyards chewed penny candy, had candy spread out careful on green grass in small, easily accessible piles.

Eliza was alarmed and tried to calm herself down, slow

rapid beat of her heart, startled in and out of her breath. People liked candy, everyone, especially kids and nothing out the ordinary about seeing a whole bunch of people eating candy early afternoon before dinner. Chewy tough candy hidden under the tongue like children hiding peppermints under the tongue at church, mouths always puckered and colored from brightly colored sugar, hands always sticky wet attracting lint and small pieces of paper.

Chocolate candy bars and red sugar lollipops and different sized and shaped penny candy sold out at the convenience store and the market. Eden ate candy like the world coming to an end and eating candy the only way to hold Heaven and earth together. Eliza ignored the demands and pleas of her girls, screwed her face up tight from the candytart taste of her husband's tongue and lips each time they kissed, tried not to stare at grown men sucking at lollipops like lollipops the same as any body part belonging to an unbearably pretty woman.

Eliza made her rounds to different households, distributed peppermint and anise tea to curb the appetite for sweets, made healthy cookies and desserts with little or no sugar and handed them out to children ruining their teeth with penny candy. Took her weeks to visit each family, scare each child with stories of old people who couldn't eat anything at all because they didn't have a tooth in their head. She started to see less and less people with candy in their hands, chocolate smeared across their faces, thought the problem under control until she noticed the melting eyes of women, the demanding and arrogant eyes of men.

Desire for sweets transferred, at least by adults, into desire for warm touch and soft kisses and love ever after. Women walked through Eden confused, smell of butter and sugar a link to every little girl fantasy about princesses and feel good touch that there ever was. Men strutted through Eden, confidant and sly, smell of butter and sugar reminding them just how easy it was to steal cookies from the cookie jar. Eliza never saw so much nonsense in her life, husbands leaving wives and wives having affairs with high school boys and teenagers burning their names in each other's skin with fiercely moving pencil erasers. Each night after dinner and the children in bed someone at her door asking how to manipulate or find love like love simple and easy if wanted bad enough. Women came dressed in form-fitting dresses and hair done, knocked at the door impatiently. She opened the door for them, perfume on their skin and lingerie hidden under form-fitting dresses and melting eyes.

They chewed nervously at nails, twisted and pulled at elaborately done and styled hair. She stepped on the porch with them, watched heat jump from their eyes, smolder and glow beneath their clean and well-oiled skin.

"Eliza, you got something for me?"

"What you need?"

She spoke to them in soft tones like she used on her children to put them to bed because the women seemed that fragile, that far gone.

"You know what I need. Just a little something to make him stay a little longer in the mornings, come over a little earlier in the evenings. Hold me a little longer, talk to me. Come on now, you a woman. You know what I need."

"I can't do that."

They laughed at her, the way grown people laughed at stubborn children.

"You cute, you really are. You and I both know that you certainly can do that."

Eliza swatted lazily at biting bugs, smiled patient and slow.

Eden, Ohio

"It's not right to make somebody do those things if it's not in their heart. It's not right and nothing good comes out of it. You don't know, really, what you asking me for."

Women raised perfectly arched eyebrows, looked her up and down like she was somebody's maid.

"You saying I'm too stupid to know what I want, Eliza? I know you not because I know you, girl. We come from the same place."

Eliza's temper was always slow to start and she simply felt sorry for women knocking on her door at night with desperation on their breath.

"I know you know me. I don't think you one bit of stupid. And I'm telling you, I can't do anything for you that we both won't regret later."

Eliza knew she could tell them about the other women she tried to help years and years ago. Mae, who didn't want her husband to leave for the horizon and new start, came to her crying and hysterical. Eliza helped her and her husband didn't leave—he fell off the roof of their house while cleaning gutters, never walked again. Sheryl, who didn't want her husband to look at anyone else and he didn't, but only because for no apparent reason he suddenly went blind.

Women rolled their eyes, sucked their teeth, sighed low in their throats.

"You won't help me?"

"I won't. Listen to me, what you're asking me is just not a good thing."

"Yeah? Where your husband at?"

"William? He's upstairs waiting on me. Why?"

Women laughed, mean nasty laugh like a slap in the face.

"I wonder why that is? I wonder why your husband come home to you each and every night while the rest of us got to worry and pray over ours. Yeah, I wonder why that is."

Women stomped down from her porch and Eliza went back to bed and worried and worried because love no children's game, nothing simple or quick or easy to understand. She got up in the mornings and walked her children to school and did her errands and watched stunned because people in Eden wasting away. Need for love hungry and insatiable burning without any kind of beloved, any kind of dream lover from movies and televisions turned inward, burned flesh and bone like racing wildfire.

Butter and sugar haze in the air from the Sweet Cake factory and the smell in clothes and hair and skin and DNA and everyone wanted voluptuous sweetness, decadent fullness that just wasn't possible in day-to-day life.

Eliza waited to see if things calmed down, if women came to their senses, lost melting eyes and wasted bodies, if men stopped strutting about cocky and arrogant, believing themselves to be kings of kings, princes instead of paupers. Things just got worst and then the first woman died, Stella. She had went to school with Stella, and Stella died from heart sickness—unbearable, unquenchable yearning in her bed waiting for her man to come home from his other woman's house. Eliza knew enough was simply enough.

She waited until nighttime, until her children in bed and William sleep deep and steady next to her. She got out of bed, dressed quietly in the dark, snuck out the house, closed the door gently behind her. She drove the car to the Sweet Cake factory, highway almost completely empty, no one on the road but her. She parked along the side of the road because the Sweet Cake factory parking gated and closed for the night. She pulled out her bag, ran her hands over fine grains of white powder Mama taught her to make for protection, to keep things contained and controlled. No more knocks at her door in the middle of the night, no more women with melting eyes, no more men trying to become dreams, no more deaths from people burning up and wasting away. She walked around the Sweet Cake factory three times, fine grained white powder falling slow from her hands, steady prayer like music playing from her lips:

> *I cried unto the Lord with my voice; with my voice unto the Lord did I make my supplication.*
> *I poured out my complaint before him; I showed before him my trouble.*

Chapter Seven

In the summer of 1986 rain chased Jeremiah out of Brooklyn. Rain polished dirty streets until streets nothing more than endless sheets of dark glass, rain kept dirty pigeons off sidewalks, rain left New Yorkers wet and soggy and even more disgruntled than ordinary traffic filled nonstop days. Rain sometimes falling hard and sometimes falling soft but never, ever stopping.

Jeremiah tried not to leave his apartment. Daddy came by most days for dinner with all kinds of ethnic food—Thai, Jamaican, Indian, Mexican, and they sat in his not bright, no window kitchen at his small table trying to hold conversations that didn't fall, always without warning, apart at the seams, didn't unravel like shirts sewn together by unsure hands. Daddy big and lanky and dark and still 1950s cool, stylish hats, cigarettes in antique case or hanging from horn-playing lips, tailored slacks and shirts, his music escaping from his throat in a steady hum.

Raining now for over two weeks with no break and weathermen on the evening and afternoon and morning news puzzled because how long? How long could rain with no end in sight last? Didn't affect Jeremiah as much as children desperately longing to run the streets, men and women on their way to work on buses and trains and cars that crawled in all the traffic.

Jeremiah had nowhere to go everyday, nowhere to be, no one waiting on him at all. He stared at himself endlessly in the mirror. He was named after his great-grandfather, Jeremiah Baker, and he had his great-grandfather's face. The only time he left the house was to visit his therapist, which he didn't mind, and for his weekly appointment and he hated going, hated getting dressed and combing his hair and making sure his legs and arms and face well lotioned to hide some of the gray beneath his brown skin. Weekly appointments the same old same old, people smiled at him like he was going to live forever and he knew for a certainty life eternal not possible for anyone, especially him.

Daddy came over around six each night, Daddy on time since Mama kicked him out the house, kicked him out the entire state of Ohio for getting days and nights confused, singing and partying like responsibility of house and wife and children something other people had to worry about, not him. Daddy let himself in with the key he had since well before never ending rain began, when Jeremiah had days he couldn't make it to the door and back to bed or the living room sofa, any place soft and willing to hold his body.

Daddy came in whistling, feet keeping beat while he walked around the small apartment turning on lights, getting plates and cups and knives and forks for dinner. Daddy hollered into the bedroom for him, sometimes woke him from easy sleep.

"Jeremiah? I'm here, man. Jeremiah, come on and eat."

The kitchen that faded into the living room and the rest of the small apartment almost too bright for him, his bedroom kept dark or lit dim by bedside lamps for reading or staring thoughtfully at walls. His life didn't require much at this point, sometimes food, very little light, very few people and he hoarded his small pleasures greedily, careful with most things his.

"Hey, Daddy. What you got tonight?"

Jeremiah was a man well grown and unable to call his father anything but Daddy, mouth and mind somehow couldn't make the transition to the more simple and adult Dad, or the cool and peerlike Pop. Daddy kissed him on the forehead, took a step back to inspect him like he did each and every day, like within twenty-four hours huge, impossible change in him.

"You look good today, man. Real good."

"At least I got dressed. What you got?"

Jeremiah sat down at the leaning-to-one-side table. Daddy went and got a phone book to make the table even.

"I was in the mood for Jamaican. Got some curried chicken, rice and peas, plantains, and rum cake. Also got a few bottles of Jamaican Kola."

"I'm starving, I didn't eat at all today, didn't realize how hungry I was until just now."

Daddy dished out food onto plates, paused to stare at Jeremiah like he was six years old and stealing the last of the cookies before everyone in the house had some.

"Jeremiah. You're messing up. You know you're messing up. You need to eat three meals a day, three good meals. I need to come over and start bringing you breakfast and lunch, too?

Unexpected conversational unraveling, he ran right into it, provided the perfect lead in, should have seen it long coming. Conversations now like war fields, thousands and thousands of landmines scattered throughout. He was always tiptoeing and pausing and holding his breath, trying to avoid getting blown up, nothing left of him. He was always the first to apologize or make things better like Daddy some delicate lace table cloth he constantly needed to be gentle with, smooth out with warm hands all the rough spots and wrinkles. Jeremiah waited in the silence, the moment stretching out like a long victory run for Daddy and he imagined Daddy strolling across well-tended fields with roses cradled in his hands and garlands of flowers wreathing his head.

"Daddy, I'm the doing the best I can."

"I know. But for me, for your mama, and brother . . . Man, for you, you need to do better."

Jeremiah shoved curry chicken and rice and peas and plantains in his mouth, chewed slowly, wondered how long he could hold off another question and response. He was fresh out of both, didn't know anymore what people who loved him wanted to hear, what he should tell them. No way for him to carefully examine, pick and choose the best, the least hurtful words when none of it good. Nothing that could possibly come out of his mouth what anyone wanted to hear.

"I played a set last night with a couple of young cats and, man, let me tell you . . ."

Daddy still a working musician, still hung out and played in clubs, still on a whole bunch of people's albums, music his first and most faithful love. Daddy went on and on about how people starting to get back into live jazz and blues, and no big surprise with all the synthesized mess attacking people from radio stations, music so filthy and so absolutely soulless Daddy worried about the children. Children when grown not being able to say, "I remember where I was and who I was with when this song came out" because songs all sounded the same, didn't lend themselves to sweet, distinctive memories. Daddy a storyteller, gift he passed down to all three of his sons. Daddy talked about hot room filled with music and humidity and Jeremiah saw sweat making lovely done up women's faces shine, sweat crawling slow and seductive from their hairlines, down the slender brown or yellow or red sides and backs of their necks, like small slivers of lemon or cherry-drop candies between their breasts and legs.

Women to Jeremiah like random sweet surprises just wandering about the world, every woman different so he never knew what he was going to get. Walking up and down the streets of Brooklyn, beautiful women so plentiful, like mangos and bananas anywhere in the Caribbean, taken for granted. Even now with weekly appointments and no good news it was hard for him to blame women as a whole or any one woman because, as his therapist so brutally quick to point out, none of it anyone's fault but his own.

He kept his mouth full, difficult to talk chewing chicken and rice and peas and plantains, no need to respond with mouth full, just gave nods when Daddy's voice paused. Daddy talked like he was trying to make up for being banished from Ohio when Jeremiah was a boy. Daddy packed up records and books and clothes and left three stunned and crying at night when nobody around boys behind and Mama relieved when the front door closed shut behind him the last time. Father-son time reduced to every other summer.

He stilled remembered the Greyhound bus rides back and forth from Eden to Brooklyn, still remembered Mama packing food and ironing clothes and buying new underwear for the two month visit. Daddy waited at the Port Authority for them when the bus pulled in, nervous and reading their faces as they got off the bus to see if he was still loved, still respected, still Daddy. First two weeks nothing more than a feeling out process. Pete, his older brother, calling Mama

every night to make sure she was fine and trying to help
Daddy adjust to having three small children constantly underfoot. Pete always tried to make everything comfortable
and easy for everyone else, always wanted the world, people to be kinder than capable. Quincy, the oldest of all, ran
wild as soon as his feet hit New York City concrete.

The food on his plate almost gone and he was thinking
about words, sentences, what he needed to say to keep their
conversation from exploding, leaving both of them without
lips, tongue, teeth. Tried to make a brief mental list, but so
many phrases had to be scratched out, so many words just
waiting to hurt Daddy, leave him acutely uncomfortable or,
even worse, painfully sad. Burden of being someone's child, a
father's son sat heavy in his gut along with half-digested curry
chicken and rice and peas. He thought, when he was a boy and
good and tired of being bossed around, picked and prodded,
being an adult must be easy, being a parent, with your own little clones like slaves, great. He knew better now, no easy in
childhood, no easy in adulthood, no easy anywhere at all.

"You got a gig tonight, Daddy?"

Daddy removed plates from the table, rolled up sleeves of
his beautifully tailored shirt to start on dishes and clean the
kitchen.

"Nope. Got a kind of date tonight."

Jeremiah got up, pushed Daddy away from running
water in the sink, running water hitting congealed dish liq-
uid and producing dingy baby bubbles.

"I can do dishes. Sit down and have some of that rum
cake you brought. What you mean, a kind of date?"

Daddy sat back down at the table, watching him carefully like doing dishes an unexpectedly dangerous task, wiping damp cloth over two dinner plates and two glasses and
two forks and knives enough to cause his lungs to stop

pumping air and his heart to stop pumping blood for good and always.

"You know. She, her name's Denise, don't think it's a date."

"What she think it is, then?"

"She thinks we just friends going out, hitting a few hangout spots. I'm going to try and convince her otherwise. Not a date but it could be. Man, it could turn out to be a lot of things I'm hoping."

"You be careful with those women."

Daddy laughed.

"Now ain't that the pot calling the kettle black."

Daddy full from food, comfortable and easy, stepped on conversational landmine. Jeremiah finished with dishes, went back to the table to watch the aftermath of shock and horror drift like black smoke from raging house fire across Daddy's face.

"Daddy, don't worry about it."

"I didn't mean it the way it sounded."

"I know you didn't."

"I come by here every day and every day I managed to say something stupid. And it's not like this all just started. It's been about what, four years?"

"Five years, more or less."

Daddy reached for his hands across the table. He was good and grown and his hands still smaller than Daddy's.

"I'm sorry, Jeremiah."

"Daddy, you've been coming by bringing me dinner every night since March and here it's the end of June. You don't have nothing to be sorry about. You doing more than enough and I thank you."

"Never no thank you between us, baby boy."

"All right, Daddy."

Daddy let his hands go, pushed back from the table,

looked around the apartment for the umbrella he left by the front door.

"Okay. So I'm going to get out of here. Can't keep Miss Denise waiting. You need anything?"

"Nope, I'm good."

"You sure you cool?"

"I'm cool."

"All right, then. I'll see you tomorrow."

Daddy let himself out and locked the door.

Apartment still with Daddy gone and Jeremiah went back to the bedroom, back to his unmade bed, sheets, blankets, pillows kicked haphazardly to the floor. His bed dipped in the center, spot permanently molded from the weight of his body and he let himself sink into that familiar space, yellow cotton sheet cool against his skin. Shades up and dark and gray outside and rain tapping, tapping unceasingly at the window, Brooklyn washed clean, all the filth of the gutter running down city sewers.

Jeremiah laid quiet, stared out the window and thought of home, thought of Eden. Home and no skyscrapers, no bridges connecting island to main land, no brownstones or designated city parks, no rush-hour traffic that never slowed down, no children sitting on their stoops with dolls and board games or jumping rope or throwing footballs in the middle of the street because nowhere else for them to play. In his apartment in Brooklyn now for just under ten years and he still felt like he was just visiting, like he had a Greyhound ticket to Eden waiting patiently to be used. He stayed away from Eden at first because New York one of the best good times. First five years in Brooklyn his life one continuous party, dance clubs and women, music clubs and women, house parties and more women. So many women coming and going, breezing in and out, busy and professional and hair and nails done and bodies young and tight from working out at gyms placed strategically at every street corner.

Coming from Ohio to Brooklyn the women astounded him, pretty and bohemian, pretty and professional, pretty and athletic, pretty in so many different ways but for all of them pretty a second job. He liked to look, liked more to touch soft butter skin and thick natural or permed straight hair, but he was always making them more comfortable in his head. Always removed high-heeled shoes and let them go about barefoot, washed off layers of makeup and let them walk around with fresh faces, used his hands to find and massage all the hurt rooted deep in beautiful brown bodies, falling like spittle from beautiful full painted mouths.

Jeremiah used to women, adored women, Eden full of surrogate grandmothers and play aunts, women feeling sorry for Mama because she had no family. All the old women in Eden determined the Baker family long since cursed and nothing for them to do but gather around, provide shelter, cushion the blows. Jeremiah grew up in old women's houses smelling like fresh baked bread and cookies and cakes. Helped old women carry shopping bags from their cars to the house, mowed lawns and helped plant gardens. He and his brothers went to church with Mama each and every Sunday, Mama had them convinced that if they missed a day they were surely committing an unforgivable sin, and in church nothing to smell but women's perfume, nothing to see but women with hats tilted jauntily to the side, dresses cleaned and pressed, faces and hands and feet done. Sweet smelling, colorfully dressed church women with hard peppermint candy hidden deep in their purses, ultimate reward for sitting still without fidgeting or giving Mama too hard a time through service.

Jeremiah carried all that love, all that good feeling and respect with him to Brooklyn, packed in suitcases, in pants pockets and wallets, and the soles of his shoes. All that love dripped from him like soft ice cream from cones on hot summer days and he was sticky with love. Beautiful Brooklyn, Queens, Long Island, Harlem, Manhattan women saw him coming, froze like small furry animals caught defenseless and bemused on busy highways, just managed to scurry out of his way, didn't know how to respond to a man who didn't want them done up, didn't want them perfect and professional, didn't want them artistic and free, just wanted them.

Jeremiah was like the plague strolling through New York City, women avoided him that hard. He learned to gather all that love dripping from him, gather all his memories of women still in Eden, stored it all in a box marked "open at later date," gave New York City women whatever it was they wanted. He was too good at it, far too good. He used to work as a graphic designer and he could play professional. He loved literature, any and every kind of art, he could play bohemian. Sometimes he was warm and caring, sometimes cold and distant, sometimes shy and reserved, whatever the woman at the time seemed to require. Nothing but fun at first, his personal life his own cheap afternoon talk show, his own soap opera. Women coming and going and going and coming and by the time he figured out how exhausting the game it was too late and he was crying to his therapists, had weekly appointments where no one in white overcoats ever had anything good to say.

No eternal life anywhere, not for anyone but New York was not a good place to fade away into the sunset—eating dinner with Daddy each night, tripping and stumbling over words, rain continuous and sky gray and charcoal, nothing at all to see on the streets from his bedroom window.

He was going home.

Chapter Eight

Aspasia woke up with Jeremiah on her mind even though she had been dreaming feet eating up long stretches of tar or dirt, highways heading toward cities, little narrow streets heading toward backwoods and thick green. In the dream she wasn't sure if it had been her or Jeremiah doing the running, the only concrete feel to the dream the overwhelming urge to get gone as far as possible. She turned over in the bed and faced the long length of Pete's muscled back. He was one of the only two men she ever loved in all creation. The other was Jeremiah, Pete's brother. She touched the warm skin of Pete's back, thought about the different ways that women loved men. Pete was the father of her baby, sturdy like bricks stacked carefully on top of each other for a house, a solid foundation. Jeremiah was her childhood friend, her best friend. The tale of their relationship told by numerous scrapes and scars on her knees and legs. She still remembered the day he left Eden for good, how all the windows in the house sweated tears even though it was early fall and the day cool.

Aspasia kissed the bare skin of Pete's back, got out of bed

and quietly dressed. Jeremiah's face, his slow smile still crowded her vision and she paused to say a quick prayer. "Keep him safe and, please, bring him home. Just one last time bring him home."

Aspasia shared the house with Pete and their child, Lula. Lula with soft brown skin, utterly smooth, like bright colorful Christmas or birthday wrapping. Baby skin smelled of fresh fruit, like Lula had peaches and apples instead of flesh. Lula part of her since conception, Lula scooted and squirmed around inside her for nine months, Lula constantly sucked at her breasts until she got tired of the mess, tired of all that grasping and gasping and slurping and put her on the bottle. First week they brought her home Aspasia's nipples chapped and bleeding, scabbed over and no way to stop it, no way to sit Lula down and say, "No. I can't do this with you right now. Hurts too much. You're going to have to try and work something else out."

Aspasia had cried each time the baby at her breasts, only lasted a week before she went out and brought formula.

Aspasia went downstairs and out the house, on her way to Lake Erie. She ignored deep chill of early day, left Lula and Pete still in bed. She started her day standing on the porch of the house, skin bumped and beaded from the cold. She left the porch, left whitewashed wooden chairs and floors, walked through town. Sky deep midnight, slashes of purples and pinks and blues, Eden a small piece of the world, winding, quiet roads, mostly single homes, green lawns.

Sun melted away remains of dark skies, huge and bright and warm. Sun skipped across pavements and front yards, sun laughed shadows on the sides of houses, overhanging branches of trees, front porches. No rain now for days and days running into weeks and weeks running into months.

Grass on front lawns brown and dry, children ran around without shirts, mandatory restrictions about when to wash cars and clothes and dishes. Pets and wild animals made lazy and listless, found some patch of shade somewhere and stayed put, ticks and fleas and mosquitoes embedded in the skin, buzzing insect clouds about the nose and mouth. The whole town wilted and curled in on itself under all the heat, whole town melted and slipped into some kind of collective deep sleep.

Butter and sugar in the air from the Sweet Cake factory a half hour from town along the highway. Butter and sugar made air heavy and dense, butter fumes settled on grass and houses and skin, made houses gleam and skin soft like women and men and children in Eden slathered moisturizer on all day. The majority of people in town worked at the Sweet Cake factory, but butter and sugar fumes in the air stunned visitors—they sat on sidewalk curbs with heads in hands or hands used as a filter covering nose and mouth.

Lake Erie hidden just beyond the marsh of growing green surrounding the town, a bit of a walk from the quiet house, sleeping man and baby. Lake Erie empty because still so early, no one on the beach or in the water. The water murky and far from clear and Aspasia measured the brown of her skin against the water's darkness.

She took off her sneakers, walked to the edge of the beach. Took off the rest of her clothes and took out her hair, hair framed her face like petals of a giant sunflower. She walked into the water, baptized and cleansed of all sins. She came up and hair plastered to her head as water cried down her.

Aspasia turned on her back, treaded water, gentle motions of her hands keeping her afloat. She thought of Lula with tiny hands and feet, her face in miniature, and felt her feet moving quick over tar paved streets, felt tar hot against her soles after baking in the sun all day long and she didn't even care because she was going. Roads, millions and thousands of roads going everywhere, small towns and huge cities and beaches with salt water and grass stretching endless across land. She knew Jeremiah had ran, the same way she wanted to run, and nothing good had come of it. That didn't stop her from wondering or waking up from dreams with her feet swollen from walking subconscious miles. Mama and Daddy long since dead, Lula and Pete and Eliza held her to this place, this small town, the same people day in day out, nothing ever changing except the seasons and no mysteries or surprises even there—winters always cold and summers always hot.

She wasn't like her sister, Eliza, didn't have magic and mystery running thick in the blood, wasn't able to look at the world and shape it into what ever it was she wanted it to be, she wasn't firstborn.

Aspasia's eyes closed, behind her lids dancing images of men before Pete. Eden didn't lack for men, men who wanted her and men who needed her and men who wanted to hurt her. All of the men, and most of the women in Eden capable of intentional cruelty at any time. It scared her as a teenager, that lust and love and pain like pieces of a jigsaw puzzle that no one in Eden could quite put together. She knew from experience, from first boyfriends and high school boyfriends before Pete waiting after school to stick tongues in her mouth and move them around like frantic animals backed in the corner. She knew they were waiting to run hands over her breasts and down her hips while she, at least as a teenager, waited for something like pleasure to kick in. She understood, each time they touched her she was putting her life in their hands—they were capable of hurting her at any given moment. The promise of feel good with eyes closed touch like she read about in romance novels and watched on television shows in which teenagers drove their own cars was enough to risk the danger.

Aspasia liked them best in the beginning, when lovers not loved like new places to discover, virgin and unknown. Men before Pete distances to be traveled, satisfied her desire for new places, new sights and distractions. Pete simply her destination, arrived at far too early, before the journey really even got underway.

Men before Pete beautiful in the beginning, sprawled across beds and floors, draped over armchairs and sofas, limbs supple and strong, elegantly defined muscle through-out the body, warm skin

When she had ended it they followed her to super-markets and parks and libraries. Louie, man she spent nights and days within his apartment just at the edge of town, just where the town dropped off and turned into long stretch of highway, tried to cut her throat. Cornered her in the alley behind Mr. Tommy's speakeasy where she went every now and then to sip a little corn liquor. His knife to her throat and warm night air, because it was the beginning of summer, the first shock of heat, rubbed against her skin. The knife cool and Louie's pleasant brown face scrunched in on itself, mouth pinched, eyes narrowed and wet for her.

"Why you going to do me this way, Aspasia? Why you going to do me like this and all I ever wanted was be with you?"

She tried to swallow but the cool knife against her throat kept anything from going down. Knife against her throat and all the nights and days spent in his apartment filled her head. Nights and days laughing and touching and holding and she had wanted him, but not always. She knew the problem somewhere between the always and sometimes.

Her hands warm on his wrist, the wrist holding the knife, fingers getting reacquainted with the feel of him. Louie way past drunk and she was sorry for him and sorry for herself, guilt making her tender.

"Come on, Louie. You don't want to hurt me. I know you don't want to hurt me."

His wet eyes on her, filled and overflowed, tracks on his cheeks. "What did I do? How come you don't want me no more?"

Her chest caved in on itself, her fingers clenching and unclenching around his wrist. Warm night air licked at her like wet dog tongue, and she wanted warm night air to lick away Louie's hurt, lick away her guilt.

"It's all right, Louie. It's all right. Go on and put the knife down."

Knife dropped from his fingers and fell to concrete. He was in her arms, his brown pleasant face crumpled, his tears and snot against her neck.

"I love you. You know I love you. I didn't mean it, didn't mean any of it."

She patted his back like he was her child. Patted his back and rocked like between her arms all the space of the world, enough to hold everyone and everything from multitudes of small ants racing beneath earth to brightly colored birds hanging still in the sky.

Her arms crowded with Louie, Louie filling up all the space, leaning into her like she had no choice but to support his weight.

"Hush now. I know. I know. Let me get you home."

Hard to be sympathetic when she still felt the blade pressed lightly against her throat, like late-night summer breezes gently tickling her skin or small summer bugs becoming drunk off her perfume and sweat. She thought about days spent in his apartment, though about the cheese sandwiches he fixed for her, thought about his hands tracing the faint stretch marks across her ass from a rushed puberty like stretch marks interesting and sexy tattoos. Louie not crazy, not insane, the knife against her throat some kind of accident she could explain once she sat down, took a minute to think everything through. She knew Louie since before memory, knew his people and parents. Something about her, huge something about Eden that made people use violence like hissing snakes against each other or themselves.

She loaded him up in her piece of a car. He cried all the way back to his place, cried and talked, good and drunk and profound with it.

"I knew you was with someone. I knew it. I just thought I could love you enough . . . I don't know. I'll just leave you alone now. No more craziness. Holding a knife to your throat? My God, I'm sorry. I'm sorry. You hate me?"

The streets like some kind of ghost town. Just a few teenagers sat on front porches, hands covering cigarettes while they smoked so mama or daddy wouldn't see. Louie rambled on and on, his face starkly visible and pitiful only when they passed beneath glaring streetlights. Louie's face fading in and out and she wanted to put her hands over his mouth.

"I don't hate you. Just be still, now. Be still."

Aspasia dropped Louie off and he left her alone. Smiled at her when he saw her on the street, kept his distance, need like cologne drifting from his skin so she was always quick to get out of his way. Never said a word, never bragged about running hands up the back of her thighs or kissing the child soft space between her shoulders and neck. Pete knew nothing about kisses and touched not received from him, never asked and didn't care. Pete was in her skin and bones and hair and it was sometimes hard for her to recall time before Pete, before Lula. So she dreamed, Pete reached too soon, other places and things for her to see and she didn't know how to backtrack on a path never traveled.

The sand was beneath her feet, she left the lake, pulled clothes over her wet body, they clung and dripped like towels wrapped beneath the underarms or the waist after a long hot shower or bath. She found a smooth rock to sit on while braiding her hair. Hair tangled and sand and who knew what all entangled in the mass—she was going to have to wash it when she got home. Stand under running water and soap her head over and over until dirt and whatever else stumbling down the bathtub drain.

Hawk Eye wandered along Main Street as Aspasia walked home. Hawk Eye a few years older than her, they went to school together all their lives, and he looked long past middle age. There was gray scattered throughout black hair and lines like crevices along the corners of his eyes and mouth. When they were children Hawk Eye was friends with Jeremiah and, by default, her friend as well. They had played together all throughout Eden and in the green surrounding town. They had learned, all three together, that the world was capable of falling all to pieces at any moment.

Hawk Eye was now always running through the streets, sometimes along the busy highway just outside of town like he wasn't flesh and blood at all, in no danger of bones crushing and breaking, cars and Greyhound buses dragging him. All roads, as many as Hawk Eye's tired feet in worn out sneakers, were his domain. He raced back and forth between sidewalks, a perfected jaywalker, dashed out from behind parked cars to loud horns and cursing.

Hawk Eye walked up to her, falling in step beside her like they were children again, contemplating how to spend a long summer day.

"Hey Aspasia."

Aspasia didn't mind the company at all.

"Hey, Hawk Eye. How you been?"

"All right. No complaints."

"Getting into anything?"

"You know. This and that."

"Yeah. Well, maybe it'll rain today. I can't stand all this heat. What you think?"

"You know I don't know. Go watch the news. Catch you later."

Hawk Eye raced in zigzag lines down the middle of the street, shirt stuck to him with sweat and the day still new. Aspasia knew Hawk Eye's name was Keith. Everyone called him Hawk Eye now like his mama didn't name him good and proper. He was a junior, named after a daddy who never wanted any parts of him. He was a man with a few kids here and there, a man who used to work the same job in and out. Now he was nothing but Hawk Eye.

When she got home Pete and Lula sitting on the front porch. Lula was crawling around on smooth wood that Pete had sanded down so no splinters waiting in silent menace for Lula's smooth and baby fat hands. Lula moved slow, stooping to sit up, look around. Her crawling was old, she was walking now and still a shock to look around and find Lula gone from where she was left. The big old house all of a sudden a dangerous place, smoothly polished hardwood floors long roads of ice, cabinets chambers of torture, stairs nothing less than death traps. Aspasia wondered how in the world to keep Lula safe until she reached eighteen or some semblance of adulthood when at a year Lula nothing more than one big accident waiting to happen. Lula brown and round and laughing, a huge butterball slowly rolling and giggling from one end of the porch to the other, thick hair a halo of baby soft nappy curls around her head.

Pete dressed in long, hot pants, white T-shirt. He was on his way to work, to the construction site, just waiting for her to get home. He knew she liked early mornings to herself, knew she liked to swim and wander and dream when almost everyone within fifty miles asleep and morning air cleaned fresh by late-night mist and dew. She knew Pete long before memory like Louie, knew him inside out because she loved Jeremiah. They were all children together playing in the playground, fighting over toys and which games, teenagers hugged up in somebody's basement while mama and daddy upstairs slow dragging.

They spent long nights talking, with Lula sleep beside them. Lula curled into her side or hiding under Pete's armpit. Pete as familiar to her as her skin and they didn't run out of things to talk about, the whole world new to Pete each day he opened his eyes. Each day something fascinating and amazing happening to him in a town where Aspasia was sure nothing fascinating or amazing happened to anyone. Pete came home from work with stories about millions of fireflies like firecrackers in the sky, romantic courtships of stray dogs in the street, birds who followed him up on half-done roofs and sang songs to him all day.

"Hey."

His voice smooth like something warm and hot going easy down the throat to sit quietly in the stomach and warm the blood. Pete tall and brown and muscles falling out of his shirt from construction work all year round, even when snow on the ground, deep and thick.

She sat down on the porch beside him, knees touching, her dripping shorts leaving a wet stain high on his thigh. He didn't pull away, moved closer to her. Lula laughed and screamed, slowly rolling and giggling over to her, stopping and starting, easily distracted.

"Hey yourself."

"Jeremiah called this morning after you left. He's coming home."

Pete played with his baseball cap, twisting and bending, fingers and hands trying to find the original shape.

Big old black ant crawled fast over Aspasia's ankle and lower calf, she brushed him quickly and gently away, watched him fly down two steps, gain his balance, run.

"You know, I woke up thinking about him. Good or bad?"

"I'm not sure. We'll see when he gets here. Nothing to do but wait. I need to call Mama and let her know he's coming. He'll most likely stay here. You mind?"

Jeremiah was still a little boy to Aspasia, still running around with scraped knees and dirty elbows, all kinds of mess embedded in his hair because he was so tender headed and rarely let anyone get a comb near him. Jeremiah playing in the yard, running down to the playground at the park, hunting for fish and any kind of floating thing in the muddy creek behind the high school. He had changed, the same way that she and Hawk Eye had changed trying to bury horror so deep that it became commonplace.

"You know I don't mind. Hope it's good, though."

"We'll see. Nothing we can do either way."

"I'll tell Eliza. See what she can do."

"You think your sister can fix anything?"

He was teasing her. She rolled her eyes.

"You and I both know Eliza could make the waters of the sea part if she wanted to."

"Yeah, you right."

Sharon from next door ran out her house, shirt limping from skirt, hair slipping from braids, on her way to the Sweet Cake factory. The Sweet Cake factory sat silent and lonely in the empty green surrounding town, millions and millions of bugs flying overhead, trying to gobble up butter sugar air. Sharon came home with hands so soft flesh like Jell-O, laughing because the flesh of her hands hidden by gloves all day, from early morning to late afternoon.

Sharon waved, rushed, called out to them.

"Good morning. Aspasia, I'll stop by after I get home from work."

Sharon drove her new car, black and shiny with care, away from them.

Pete waited on his ride, waited on Red's pickup truck to come flying down the road. They took turns, each week a different hand at the wheel, a different truck eating up highway. Aspasia knew Pete liked to ride best, riding didn't take any kind of concentration, allowed him to stare out windows, study and pick apart all the mysteries in the world just waiting for him. Red Cap was driving today and Pete wasn't looking forward to it one bit because Red Cap dangerous and unpredictable behind the wheel, any little thing capable of setting him off.

"We going back to work at the new housing development off the highway. Last time I was there I saw a few families of possum fall from trees. Fell from their homes while we were cutting them down, tumbling like they were acrobats. Some of them dead from just fright before they hit the ground."

Her hands tightened and loosened, hands felt like

Sharon's hands, swollen and damp from butter and sugar. As long as she could remember the Sweet Cake factory giving off fumes along the highway between Eden and Cleveland, Sweet Cake factory as much a part of Eden now as lush green surrounding town. The sticky sweetness always in the air settled on her upper lip, along her hairline. She wiped sweet smelling sweat away with the back of her hand, looked up into the sky, into yellow butter haze.

"I can't imagine that. It's just sad. Why would anyone want to live off a highway with nothing around anyway? Kids can't walk to school, no corner stores, got to drive to the market."

Pete's ride pulled in front of the house. Red Cap, yellow face bright with sweat and the day not even in good yet, work not even started, behind the wheel of a dirty pickup.

"How you doing, Aspasia?"

She waved.

"How's my girl?"

Aspasia lifted Lula from the porch, made fat little hands wave frantically.

"Lula waving hi, Poppop."

Pete pulled on the plait at the back of her head like their front porch the playground at grade school and a crush eating him up inside.

"It's close to the mall. See you later."

She held on to him, his shirt a little damp.

"Huh?"

"The housing development. It's near the mall."

They left Aspasia thinking about Jeremiah coming home, thinking about possums falling from trees like burning stars shooting through sky, falling dead to hard ground.

Chapter Nine

Pete rubbed his hands together, hands callused and rough from working outdoors year round. His skin made noise like sandpaper rubbing against dry wood. He had big hands, like Daddy. He didn't look anything like Daddy, Mama spit him out, but he had Daddy's hands and Daddy's eyes.

Red Cap was reckless behind the wheel, drove like no one else on the highway. Cars rode him close or beeped horns, and drivers hurled insults, sometimes cigarette butts and unrecognizable flying debris. Red Cap was unconcerned, light face ruddy from sweat, sweat always pouring from Red Cap even when snow knee-to-hip deep on the ground.

Red Cap eyed the rear view window.

"Some people too stupid to live."

"Jeremiah coming home."

Pete stared straight ahead, heat rising from the rode in slick waves.

"Your Mama know?"

"I'll call her this afternoon."

"You all let Eliza know?"

"Aspasia's going to catch up with her today."

They saw Hawk Eye walking along the shoulder of the highway, kicking at rocks and dirt, shading his eyes and looking up at the sky, sun like uncontrollable fire eating up the pure, expansive blue. Plastic Sweet Cake wrappers gathered like cheap fake flowers along the highway, carelessly thrown from cars. Red Cap slowed a little and leaned on his horn. Hawk Eye was startled, turned and waved, gave a kind of general's salute.

Red Cap just shook his head.

"Damn shame. I remember when that boy had sense. And he still a good boy, don't cause nobody a bit of trouble."

Pete stared back through the window, Hawk Eye smaller and smaller, trail of dust from kicking feet rising high about his waist. Hawk Eye walking in the dust, under the hot sun a familiar image. Pete remembered Jeremiah, Hawk Eye, and Aspasia running through the dust under hot sun as children, running so fast and so carefree that they seemed to eat up dust with open mouths as they went along. When Jeremiah left Eden for New York, Mama and all the old women in Eden became depressed, stayed in houses with shades drawn to discourage visitors and sunlight. They missed Jeremiah visiting them, sitting patient with them as they cooked him fresh bread and cookies and slowly unraveled the tapestry of their lives. And all the old men sitting on their front porches late afternoons had fewer stories to tell. They were used to Jeremiah's attentive face mirroring the wonder of their words.

"He better get out the sun. No reason to be out here if you don't have to."

The middle of a drought, the whole state dry and thirsty for water, everyone, even the children, sick of sun and heat. Pete had to put the air conditioners in the windows of the house early. Aspasia and Lula woke up soaked with wet even with all the windows in the house wide open. Lula was cranky and miserable, no way at all for her to get comfortable. Still, he and Aspasia would have tried to hold out a minute longer just to save money if Mama hadn't called.

"I rode by the house today and didn't see no air conditioners in the window. I know you don't have my grandbaby over there sweating in all this heat? You know how fragile our constitutions are?"

He told Aspasia and she laughed and rolled her eyes, his mama almost like her own.

"We better put the air conditioner in before she comes over and puts them in herself."

Mama was paranoid because people in the family just died, sudden illnesses, hit by cars, run over by trains, trampled by crowds leaving crowded high school football or basketball games, in house fires. Bakers famous in over three counties because they died often, no one left in the family but Mama and his youngest brother, Jeremiah. His older brother, Quincy, got shot down in Cleveland years ago, was brought home in a body bag with no face. The town cemetery crowded with aunts and uncles and nephews and nieces resting in peace, keeping the grass of cemetery lush and healthy.

The heat came through the vents in the car, Red Cap's truck didn't have any air conditioner and Pete tried not to think about the sweat gathering around the waist of his pants, his underarm hair slick and funky, despite deodorant, beneath his shirt.

Whenever Red Cap drove entire ride spent in long hushes punctuated by surprised sighs and sucking teeth, everyone else on the road dangerous and maybe criminal and not the slightest bit worthy of any driving courtesy. Red Cap's yellow skin baby smooth the way black men's skin get around the age of sixty or so, wrinkles carved in yellow flesh lightly, with kindness and consideration, wrinkles just kind of outlining baby smooth skin. No slight sag at the neck, no slight droop at the eye, like Mama. Not a year passed Mama by without leaving some kind of winding trail on her skin because Mama had three boys to raise and a husband gone. She spent long nights sitting in the dark talking things through with herself. Red Cap had nothing even slightly resembling a child—no dog faithfully following, no cat curled up at the foot of his bed, not even a goldfish swimming stupidly in a bowl. Red Cap ran the streets well into old age like teens and twenties lasted forever if you didn't slow down long enough for thirties and forties and fifties to catch up with you.

He was famous around town with all the boys and men because how did he do it? How did he have women living around the corner from each other and down the street from each other and sometimes right next door to each other and no kind of ugliness ever broke out. No women ran after him with tears and tantrums or any kind of sharp instrument, no women chased down each other with bats and broken bottle tops, nobody in the hospital or scared to leave their house. He asked Mama about it when old age finally made Red Cap tired and he hounded and romanced Mama until she married and moved into his big old house with him. Mama sat at Red Caps's table, her table now, while Red Cap sweet-talked neck bones and cabbage cooking at the stove.

Mama just kind of slanted her eyes at Red Cap, smiled that wide smile Pete remembered from childhood when him or anyone of his brothers did something out of the ordinary good.

"Some men know how to leave a woman with way more than he come through the door with. Sometimes it don't even hardly matter what he does when he's there or what he does when he's not there as long as he leaves you full, so full you don't hardly have energy to be evil or act the fool. That's Red Cap. I remember when he was seeing Laney, you remember that Red? And I was over at Laney's house and she called around just as calm and nice as you please to Ann's looking for Red. Red wasn't there and they talked on the phone for a minute, asking about grandchildren and children. I've never seen anything like that. Don't think any man could pull it off except Red."

Mama looked at him hard then.

"Maybe you, Pete. You got that same kind of sweetness and generosity about you. Yeah, maybe you."

Red Cap hushed her at the stove.

"Now Vern, why you going to be trying to pass on to that boy all my bad habits. I'm hardly proud of none of it."

Mama smiled at Red Cap until some of the clouds gone from his baby smooth old man's skin.

"Proud? Honey, it don't got a bit to do with proud. You lucky your yellow behind made it out breathing and all those women still kind to you, still think something good of you instead of waiting for a chance to do serious and lasting harm."

Heat wind blew in Pete's face, heat wind didn't even cool him off a little, just forced sweat rolling from his hairline to map new and exciting paths down his face. Long stretch of flat black road sprawled out ahead of them, no twists or turns, sudden dips just road going on for always. Waves rose from the road and the sun not even good up in the sky,

Pete wondered how he was going to make it until dusk when the road and town started to cool off and the fireflies came out to play in moist night air.

Red Cap messed with the tuner on the radio, one hand lightly skimming the steering wheel and the other busy with dials and knobs, DJ sugar voices yelling and fading from the speakers. Pete tried not to pay any kind of attention to Red's truck swerving slightly, tried not to count how many seconds Red's eyes followed the tuner and stayed, with a kind of belligerent defiance, off the road. Red didn't believe there was anybody left in creation that knew how to drive as well as he did—no need to worry about other cars and vans barreling through like minitanks. Pete all the time wondered why Red didn't get thrown through his front window years and years ago.

Red just laughed at him.

"Nothing going happen to me before my time, boy. You just stop wasting all your worrying on me."

Pete's forearm hung out the window, sun like a stinging slap laying into his skin and Pete tried to conjure up Mama's face if something happened to Red. Red found an oldies station on the radio and turned his gaze, with no real enthusiasm, back to the road. The station played Curtis Mayfield's "It's Alright" and Pete remembered Daddy singing Curtis Mayfield, singing and dancing all about the house, up and down stairs, on the front porch waving on beat to neighbors—Daddy singing and sometimes not going to work, Daddy singing and sometimes spending food or bill money on cards or beer. Daddy sang and forgot to come home and all that singing beat Mama down into a small, quiet old woman, no enjoyment left for her because Daddy ran around squandering it all.

Daddy was tall and brown and thin, skin hanging loose

over his tall frame waiting for muscle or fat to fill out. His mouth took up his whole face, mouth wide and most of the time smiling, teeth white against his brown skin. Daddy was a sax player and Mama said his mouth so soft and fine and wide because he took care of it like women took care of their hair, always pampering and gentle. Daddy played with his children, got down on the floor and crawled with them throughout the house, pulled pillows from couches and stacked them high for forts, created dinners from milk chocolate bars and soda pops, helped them drag toy soldiers and boats into the bathroom and filled the tub until water overflowing and leaking to the floor, another mess for Mama to clean up.

Daddy worked sometimes but home more often than not, home sitting in his underwear and watching television in the living room when they all came in from school. Daddy home all day and the house a mess and children running wild and no dinner ready when Mama came home from the Sweet Cake factory. Pete watched Mama walk through the door and pause, chew on her lip, her eyes moving slow about the room. Pete just knew she was thinking about how and why and where could she possibly go to get away from all of them, the absolute mess of her life.

The music always in the house stopped when Mama asked Daddy to leave. Mama came home from grocery shopping one Saturday afternoon after being up since early morning scrubbing floors, dusting tables, wiping down woodwork, and none of them dressed. All of them sat around in underwear in front of the television, cereal and splatters of milk trailing from kitchen to living room. Daddy watched afternoon Kung Fu Theater with them, humming his song under his breath, tapping his foot in rhythm, cleaning his horn. Pete sometimes thought that things would have been different if one of them offered to unload bags out the car, if they could have turned away from the television and the blur of hands and feet moving in dazzling displays to acknowledge that she had come into the room, if Daddy could have stopped humming just for a minute, just long enough for Mama to feel that his music wasn't all the time assaulting her. Mama brought all the bags into the house, stepped over their sprawled-out bodies on the living room floor on the way to the kitchen, never opened her mouth or even glanced in their direction.

Pete didn't hear anything that night, no slamming doors, no ugly words barreling through walls. The next morning when they went down to Sunday breakfast dressed for church Mama at the stove frying ham and Daddy at the kitchen table completely quiet, no singing, no humming, no toe tapping, no nothing. Pete and Quincy and Jeremiah couldn't figure it out at first, couldn't understand what was different and looked all about the kitchen, at the clean white walls, and the tiled lemon drop floor, the lace curtains at the window, and the sturdy oak table that Mama said had been in the family for generations but still looked new.

Mama threw them a look and her eyes were bloodred like the strawberry jam on the center of the table, her voice calm.

"Come on and eat now."

All of a sudden they were obedient children, no fuss, no fighting over chairs and who was going to sit where, the weight of whatever was different quelling all their energy, making them sit nice and still in church clothes that were too tight and itched against their skin.

Mama always made a big Sunday breakfast—grits and biscuits and fried ham and eggs. They were in church long after lunchtime because no matter how much he and his brothers prayed over it the preacher never quit preaching and the choir never quit singing, some kind of devious plot to keep children from playing.

Daddy wasn't dressed for church, sat with hands flat at the table, no plate with food piled high in front of him and no music. No music the most disturbing thing of all and Pete looked at his brothers and they all held their breaths and didn't think about touching the food Mama put down before them, waiting for some kind of sound.

Mama grew impatient with their dumb stillness, motioned slowly to their plates.

"You all go on and eat now. I'm going to get dressed for church."

She left the room and Daddy smiled at them like whatever was going on nothing to really worry about, but Pete knew better, knew that the big old house Mama's people had since just after slavery about to sway uncertainly on its foundation and crush them. His whole family beaten into dirt and dust and nothing he could do but watch Daddy's smile sour his face.

Daddy left Ohio the same way he came. His blue beat-up van chewed up long stretches of highway, grasping and greedy across the interstate all the way to Brooklyn, New York. Daddy rode into town on his way somewhere else with his Jazz quartet. Eden was not a destination on anyone's map, not a spot circled in red ink, not worth miles on the highway. Pete knew the story, Mama was almost some kind of celebrity in town because Daddy saw her drinking pop out front of the only convenience store in Eden at the time and never left, sent his quartet on without him by way of Greyhound, had babies and stayed. Mama for a long time after they married considered one of the luckiest women in town because Daddy always dressed in nice suits and shirts, shoes always shined, and hats tilted on his head. All of Eden in awe of Daddy's smooth city style. Mama always said the only reason she gave Daddy the time of day was because his last name the same as hers, both of them Bakers was just too much of a coincidence for Mama not to be some kind of fate.

New York was Daddy's hometown and Pete knew nothing about it except what he saw on television and he didn't quite trust what he saw. TV shows and news all the time made out like only white people lived in Ohio and he knew almost nothing but black folks. No way for him to be sure that New York was filled with prostitutes and pimps and Mafia, for all he knew New York could be just like the green that festered around town, green so thick and dense that children all the time getting lost and adults half-heartedly trying to beat it back. Beat back the grass and the bushes and the trees and wild flowers and keep the town proper from resembling some enchanted story forest.

Night before Daddy left they all went into the green surrounding the town. Daddy was quiet, no humming or anything at all slightly resembling music since Sunday breakfast. It was early fall and all the lightning bugs were dying, fading and falling. Daddy took them walking in the green all the time, loved the way nature took over and things sometimes blooming and sometimes dying nothing man had any kind of control over. Lightning bugs lined green beneath their feet like fluorescent carpet and Pete felt a little sad in the middle of all that death. Fall nothing at all but a season of dying, leaves rotting from trees, flowers shriveling from the cold, insects like firecrackers beneath the foot. Daddy walked in front of them and all them trying to keep up, not stumble over each other in the night.

"You all know this isn't good-bye. Just a kind of see

you later. Your Mama and me worked it out and you all can come out and see me each summer in New York. You all probably love it there. All this stuff to do, not like here at all."

"All right, Daddy."

Pete mouthed the words with his brothers, knew this was not a kind of see-you-later stroll. Hadn't he and his brothers help Daddy drag all his records from down the basement—jazz and blues and soul and Motown? Daddy loved his records almost as much as he loved his sons, probably more. Cleaned his records once a week. Brought some up from the basement cradled like a child and listened to them all day on Sundays and when he wasn't working. That evening before they left for the green Daddy sat them in the middle of the living room on the floor, records scattered like hard pillows around them.

"I want you to have this one, Quincy, 'cause you're so stubborn and this will help you mellow out. Pete, this one's for you because I know you have the patience to understand it. Jeremiah, this one's for you, I hope the drums beat some caution into that head of yours."

Pete watched Daddy dividing up records with instructions until he only had a milk crate of records to take back to Brooklyn with him. Milk crate old and torn at the sides, bright orange faded to dull, Daddy's old records seemed bare and vulnerable, not priceless just cheap. He stared at the records in the milk crate until his eyes crossed and his head hurt, tried not to think of Daddy leaving them the best he had to offer, taking nothing back with him to Brooklyn besides pictures and memories sure to grow old and stale.

His brothers sat dumbstruck and silent because what were they going to do with all those records, where were they going to put them, what toys would have to be moved around, put away? Pete looked at Daddy and tried not to cry because he knew Daddy was giving them their inheritance and he knew people didn't get inheritances unless somebody died.

Chapter Ten

Waves of heat beat at bare skin of legs and arms, heat licked at the sweat between breasts and underarms and Eliza sat on her porch and read the Bible. The New Testament and Jesus and Jehovah and Moses and King David and Adam and Eve and all Twelve Disciples a pleasant, familiar blur in her head. Eliza knew her Lord and Savior Jesus Christ, walked with him and talked with him when things not good. Belief in God the same as loving Mama and her sister, Aspasia, the same as trusting in the hands and wisdom of all the old women still living and breathing in Eden and demanding something more from life than only ordinary.

The summer felt long and it was still June. It was the heat, heat so bad dead cats and dogs scattered throughout the roads, too lazy and too tired to move out of the way of moving cars. Eliza never saw the S.P.C.A truck ride by her home so much in a short period of time, even though everyone and everything died fairly young in Eden. There were three funeral homes in Eden because funerals were good business.

Eliza looked out over her yard. She kept a garden that went from the front of the house to the back, garden started long before she was a spark in the womb, garden that would be kept when she was comfortable in the grave, faded memory. Garden was full of flowers, roses and daffodils and sunflowers and pretty wildflowers otherwise known as weeds that she let grow free. Her house surrounded by flowers and fresh flowers always at her tables and in her kitchen during the spring and summer. She grew herbs as well, lavender and rosemary, thyme and lemongrass, more herbs than flowers because knowledge of herbs in her blood, passed from mother to firstborn daughter since well before time, knowledge ancient. How to get rid of a cold and clean the system and chase bad luck away and make a sick child well and help a dead womb conceive.

She was her mama's child.

Eliza the kind of woman who carried lavender water in her purse, had scented sachets buried deep in her brassiere, made bread from scratch and kept a small vegetable garden along with her flowers and herbs. She was the kind of woman men married and still waiting at close to thirty for her man to appear, admire her garden and her wonderful self, settle in, stay awhile. Her first almost disastrous marriage terrified her so badly she was in no rush, no sly smiles gathered and aimed with skill at stunned male faces, no time for flirtation and the long leap into trust. She had children to see well and old women to make better and young girls to guide and men to make act like men, not magicians who vanished completely at the last curtain call.

Eliza hoped better for Aspasia and Pete. She knew Pete's family history, knew his oldest brother dead and his baby brother close enough. She made herbal teas and tinctures for Pete and prayed he lived long because Pete and Aspasia's love was complete in and of itself. Not like love in the rest of Eden. Love for everyone else nothing more that mirrors in a fun house, a mess of distorted images, nothing at all to be trusted.

The women ran streets from one end of the town to the other, let dresses be pulled up or shimmied down in back car seats or the green around town and needed—desperately needed—some kind of help. Just a whisper in the ear, a light caress against the neck and shoulder to slow down. Slow down because nothing in the whole wide world was as painful as constantly rushing and rushing and staying stuck in one place. Eliza saw them on Wednesday nights going to prayer meetings, strolling up and down the sidewalk, hanging on men, skirts almost showing crotch and breasts just covered. Prayed for them in her garden, like she prayed for any warm living thing, picking herbs for dinner, cutting fresh flowers for the house, trying to think of herbal teas to help her niece, Lula, get through teething and her sister, Aspasia, relax and settled into her blessings instead of always wanting more

Aspasia, the image of Mama right down to the voice and birthmark, her child since Mama died. Aspasia loved best in the world, blood of her blood and flesh of her flesh. Same memories and same things forgotten and same things held close.

Eliza didn't look anything like Mama, but she was firstborn and she had Mama's name. Mama the same as herself, and she was the same as all the Elizas before her, same as the Eliza who guided twelve families up through the South during slavery to Eden. She didn't need to look like Mama because she knew her inside out and outside in, finished Mama's sentences before words left her tongue, knew what Mama wanted or needed before Mama said anything at all.

Mama taught her how to grow flowers and herbs and vegetables, how to heal and comfort, how to hurt and seek justice. Eliza was five years older than Aspasia and when Aspasia finally came stumbling from Mama's womb Eliza grown enough to be a little mother.

Looking back now their childhood seemed lost in forever, when they were girls and Mama and Daddy smothered by each other and always fighting and always making up and finding time for hugs and kisses and family dinners in the middle of unceasing friction. They ran wild through the town like twins just separated at birth, despite the age difference, where one went the other happily and blindly followed.

Mama was so beautiful, had this air about her, made people helpless to love her. Eliza, as a little girl with long pigtails and thumb always shoved carelessly in the mouth, caught Mama and Daddy in bed on a dreary Saturday morning. She knew it was Saturday because Aspasia was curled into herself in the living room watching cartoons, sprawled out on the worn and tired sofa, waiting patiently for breakfast. Hunger like a fist in her belly made her uncurl small arms and legs away from Aspasia, leave Aspasia waiting for her with wide eyes. Forced her to climb stairs and open Mama and Daddy's bedroom door. The room quiet except for deep, uneven rush of Mama and Daddy's breathing. Hardwood floor became little girl flytrap beneath Eliza's feet because what she saw was forbidden—Mama and Daddy sent them to bed when movies showed naked bodies and roaming hands. Mama and Daddy entangled and engrossed never heard at all. The sheets a mess on the bed, long length of Daddy's back bare and Mama's smooth brown legs like milk chocolate bars against white covers.

Eliza really looked at her family; saw Mama's beauty and

strength and Daddy's charm and weakness. Aspasia was so lovely that strangers stopped in the street to stare, memorize smooth butter skin of cheeks and forehead and long little girl legs. And she, well she was an Eliza. Her entire family larger than life, walked around town like minor celebrities. Daddy always with sweet smelling women trailing after him and eyes only for Mama; Mama strutted around like a man, doing whatever she choose; Aspasia followed fast in Mama's footsteps. Everyone else in Eden, beneath the harsh light of all that brilliance, was simply ordinary.

Mama got sick when she was thirteen and Aspasia eight. At first Mama always tired, all the color left Mama's skin so she looked like the faded leather on shoes worn too long. Mama's thick, black hair thinned and fell out from the root, Mama's nails brittle and weak. Eliza left for school in the morning and Mama in bed; Eliza came home from school in the evening and Mama still in bed. Mama in bed went on for weeks and weeks and there were all these trips to the hospital.

Then Eliza and Aspasia came home from school and Mama in the hospital and Daddy at the kitchen table lost. The hospital just up the road, anywhere in town just up the road really, but Daddy talked like Mama had left the town, dropped from the edges of the world, somewhere lost in deep space. There were no more long days without worry, and running through backyards and up and down sidewalks light and easy in her skin because Mama checking on her every few minutes. Little girl with a mama in the hospital instead of at home cooking dinner and giving baths and combing hair wasn't any kind of little girl at all, just a child always afraid and always quiet because no one around to kiss away hurts and make things all better.

Eliza struck still by the enormity of Mama gone but just

down the road and Aspasia climbed in Daddy's lap, held him. Daddy clung to her small brown body, ran hands over Aspasia's nappy, thick, dark hair like Mama's. Told them Mama was dying, told them in a voice almost normal, soothing, tried to take sting out the words, make things all better. Eliza knew only mamas had all-better power and Mama good as dead, cancer and nothing anyone could do. Air chewed up and swallowed in the entire kitchen and Eliza couldn't breath. Lungs collapsed in on themselves and her hands clawed at her throat, left bloody swerving trails along the curve of her neck and upper chest. Snot dripped from her nose and tears, stung her eyes. She knew all along, Mama had told her that this was coming, but the knowledge in no way prepared her for the actuality.

Aspasia didn't get it at all, didn't understand what not having a mother meant, didn't have sense enough to know that some things only a mother could teach, could tell.

Daddy deserted them almost completely. Mama came home but the smell of death in her hair, riding her skin, lingering like peppermint candy on her breath. Smell took over the house, buried in carpets, huddled behind draperies. The smell made all Eliza's insides clench because she didn't want to be motherless and she didn't want to die and if Mama was dying that meant all of them were dying every second of every day.

Eliza visited Mama after school in her bedroom. Mama just stared out the window, wrote in a journal or read if she felt up to it, most of the time she laid on covers, eyes closed, utterly still. It hurt Mama to laugh or eat or talk or leave the bedroom upstairs and stop staring out the window for hours until the closed windows fogged up and the entire room smelled like Mama's breath. Mama didn't let them open windows, not even during days so hot hair on the head just melted into sweat, and fingernails turned soft and peeled and bled at the edges. Mama sat still, let her weight just fall off, clothes almost two sizes too big and hanging from her like the baby-doll clothes Eliza used to try to put on dolls. Mama's brown skin dull and ashy, her lips cracked, the nail polish on her finger and toenails chipped and peeling, hair wild all over head because she didn't do anything with it.

"Hey, Mama?"

Eliza whispered because Mama most of the time sleep.

Mama opened eyes no longer pretty or interested, just sad.

"Hey, honey girl. How was school?"

"It was okay. We had pizza for lunch."

Mama smiled. "Pizza, huh?"

"You feeling better?" Eliza asked the same question day in, day out.

"Don't worry about me, honey girl."

Eliza stared, wanting to go, to stay.

"You want to lay down with me? You so big you never want to lay with me no more."

Eliza went to Mama, big grown girl of thirteen, gently wrapped Mama's weak arms around her small body. She tried to ignore the sickness and the sadness. Mama's skin like raw chicken left too long on the sink to defrost when skins slid from the bones like nothing underneath. No bones and Eliza hated the feel of all that soft skin. Soft skin reminded her of old people and she wanted Mama to be young, not near death the way she thought old people were on a real friendly basis with death; just sat on their porches or laid in their beds and waited for death to come strolling along.

Aspasia stayed with Mama and read to her and talked to

her and played board games and cards, death riding Mama's skin not bothering her at all. Eliza watched Aspasia take care of Mama, watched Aspasia's hands smoothing lotion over Mama's dry skin or braiding Mama's almost-all-gone hair. Stepped back and gave Aspasia time to get to know Mama because her and Mama the same and she had Mama all to herself for five long years.

The day Mama died, bitterly cold Sunday in November, Eliza in the house of the Lord praying. Kept right on praying through the funeral, through Daddy's utter desertion from their lives even though he came home every night from work and sat through dinner with them in the kitchen. Aspasia was five years younger and more like her child than sister, Eliza washed and braided Aspasia's hair every week until she got grown enough to do it herself, made sure Aspasia had breakfast in the morning and dinner at night, sang Aspasia songs before bed and played games during the weekend. The only thing she couldn't do was drag Aspasia to church, Aspasia just refused to go and Daddy gone and yet there not able to make anybody do anything.

Eliza kept right on praying and met brother Carl when she was eighteen and Aspasia thirteen.

White faces terrified brother Carl. More than the milkiness of skin, softness like mashed potatoes or vegetables, nothing in entire whole wide world should be that soft. Horror beneath white faces scared brother Carl, the meanness, and nothing to do, no way at all for him to fight back.

Growing up in Mama's house he never really saw white people, just on television. White people on television laughing and carefree, sometimes angry and crying but even tears and rages pretty, no snotty noses, no slamming doors or ugly words. White people went places, did things, had fun.

Wasn't until he really paid attention to white people on TV that he understood the games he and his friends played after school and weekends and long summer days weren't fun at all. Fun was getting in the family car and going anywhere. Anywhere. In TV shows smiling white children randomly picked some spot off a neatly laid out map and smiling white parents said, "Okay, that's where we'll go."

Fun was going next door to swim in John's pool or spending the entire day huddled up in Bill's tree house. He didn't know anything at all about fun, never had fun a day in his life.

When he was eight he poked and prodded at Mama.

"How come we don't live near no white people?"

Mama cooked dinner and waited for Daddy to walk through the door. Kitchen walls were stained with smoke from the stove, tile of the floor missing in places, white curtains at the window just a little dingy. The kitchen was brother Carl's favorite part of the house.

"We just don't."

"But how come?"

Brother Carl sat at the table on old and wobbling kitchen chairs.

"Boy, you and your 'how comes.' Black folks and white folks just don't seem to get along like that."

"You don't like white people?"

"No, I'm not saying that."

Mama sweating and fanning herself with one hand, trying to turn pork chops with the other.

"I'm saying that . . . All right. I don't think about white folks, don't care what they do or where they live as long as they leave me and what belongs to me alone. That make sense to you?"

Brother Carl just sadly shook his head.

"But look at all the stuff they do."

Mama laughed.

"Boy, when was the last time your narrow behind talked to a white person? How you know what they do?"

"I watch TV. I know."

"Baby, that ain't real. That's like make believe."

"I think they nice, Mama."

"I guess some of them are, some of them got to be, right? But the ones I know I like to keep at arm's distance."

Brother Carl left home after high school graduation for Penn State. Blacks and whites sat on different sides of the cafeteria, had separate parties, separate clubs and organizations. It was 1975 and he was expecting things to be different, he was part of the promised generation and white folks walked around campus like they weren't even aware a promise had been made. A year at Penn State and he thought nigger was his nickname. He was called nigger in classrooms by smiling professors, nigger in study groups, nigger walking across campus, nigger in the library, nigger in the bathroom, nigger in the school paper. Different, clever words for it, but he knew what all those words meant. He started having panic attacks. Panic attacks in the middle of class with professors using big words and still calling him nigger, nigger digging into his chest.

Brother Carl's degree in hand in three years and he ran back to his mama's house, his old neighborhood and no white faces. Brother Carl joined church, worked at a black accounting firm, stopped watching television. Nigger didn't go away. Brother Carl still had panic attacks, dreams of roaming the jungle in lion's skin, dreams of Tarzan swinging through trees, riding elephants, chasing him down. He wanted a family; maybe as some woman's husband he could finally be a man. Eliza perfect because she was a lady, carried herself well, always calm, cool, like chocolate didn't melt in her mouth. She was an Eliza, known throughout Eden for generosity and healing and, some said, magic, but he didn't believe a word of it.

First time he saw her in at church, everyone else was filled and singing with the Holy Ghost, any hint of dignity gone to the Lord. Eliza sat rubbing at smooth skin along her neck with the fan that the local funeral home provided. Brother Carl set out on seduction and seduction easy because Eliza simple and trusting, inherently kind.

Eliza invited him to Sunday dinner to meet family and her daddy nowhere to be seen, but Aspasia smiling at him and taking his coat when he walked through the door. Aspasia dressed in old, worn blue jeans and faded yellow poet's blouse, hair in a thick bun on top of her head. She was still a child, not quite a woman, but he wanted whatever she had, wanted to hold her down and take it from her. She was round and brown and golden and he knew her, saw her around town with people her own age, thought she was a pretty thing but never paid much attention.

Aspasia came to the table barefoot and unconcerned, Eliza shook her head and laughed, brother Carl was amused and fascinated. All through dinner—through potato salad and candied yams and baked chicken and collard greens— he stared at Aspasia. Studied the texture and color of her skin, the span of her neck, waist and hips, waited for her smile. Looked and looked at her in all her unself-conscious blackness, all her child's easiness in her skin and the horror of white faces disappeared. The horror of his own powerlessness was gone, she robbed nigger of any importance. She was a child and made him feel like a different person, not a nigger, a man.

At dessert, eating ice cream and apple pie he tried to listen to Eliza talk about her garden. Ice cream, to tease him, fell from the spoon at Aspasia's mouth to lazily drift down her chin. Brother Carl sat right next to her and watched the ice cream linger on the smooth brownness of her skin. Eliza went to the kitchen to refill the pitcher of water and brother Carl, unable to stop himself, stood and leaned across the table, getting his own ice cream smeared across his tie, and gently, with his tongue, licked the ice cream off her chin before her hands got to it. Once his tongue actually on her he couldn't control himself and his mouth wandered along her throat, down to the tops of her breasts, settled on her mouth, where he could taste the ice cream, cool and sweet. Aspasia frantically tried to pull away from him, her hands pushing against his chest. He wrapped his arms around her, felt every bone in her child's body, energy racing just beneath her skin. She tasted like salt of the sea and over-ripe fullness of clouds and sweet/bitter flavor of early morning sun. He wanted to crawl up inside her, just stay there, curled and safe and tight.

Eliza came back to the dining room and the pitcher of water slid effortlessly from her hands, broke into shining, sharp pieces at her feet. She watched, struck dumb by brother Carl holding tight to her hysterical, fighting sister like he was sharing secrets of the old world and magically shaping, from ashes and dust, a new one. Slowly the rage built, but the rage uncertain, stunned. Aspasia blood of her blood and flesh of her flesh, her baby.

Rage came to life, twisting and clawed in her stomach. Rage rooted her to the floor, rooted her to that exact moment in time.

She didn't want to go to heaven or be saved by Jesus. She only wanted brother Carl to suffer. She wanted tears and regrets and blood, if damned to Hell she'd happily go, singing and dancing and laughing. Her mind a jumble of confusion, considered all the possibilities. Her arms wanted to reach for the carving knife and slit brother Carl's throat, feel warm blood running over her fingers, down her wrists, permanently staining her hands. She couldn't move, no control over her physical body. She clenched her hands, let them relax. The scream started way down, hidden in the maze of her intestines. Made its way through her stomach where dinner of chicken and candied yams and collard greens turned sour, climbed up her throat. Her mouth opened and her scream lifted the house and brought it crashing back down on all of them. Brother Carl jumped like her scream a gunshot or unexpected fire sirens. Aspasia pulled at her mouth like lips and tongue and teeth could all be replaced. Her baby sister violated by a man she brought into the house, man she opened her legs and closed her eyes for, man she thought she loved. She thought about Mama and Daddy all the time fighting and all the time making up, their words like grenades launched constantly throughout the house. She realized that no matter all she knew, no matter all the ways she could heal or hurt, she was still capable of terrible lapses in judgment, not quite so perfect just like Mama.

"Get out of my house. Get out of my house."

All the screaming gone, but the need to hurt him made Eliza's eyes roll in her head.

"Let me explain . . ." brother Carl frantic.

"That's my baby sister. You hear me? That's my baby. Get out."

He didn't move fast enough, Eliza grabbed the carving knife from the shell of the chicken. He was sick; Aspasia was a child, her child.

"You touch her again, I'll kill you."

"Look, it's not . . ."

"Listen good, Carl. I will kill you and not think twice about it."

Brother Carl left and Aspasia cried and pulled and pulled at her lips. Eliza just stared at her; Aspasia a child, her child. She went to her, placed hands in Aspasia's nappy hair, pulled her tear stained face into her abdomen.

"Hush now, Aspasia. You didn't do nothing wrong. I know you didn't do nothing wrong."

Eliza whispered, tenderness and love more heavy than rage like stones in her breast.

Chapter Eleven

Leaving New York was not difficult at all, Jeremiah's friends had long since disappeared into skyscrapers with air-conditioned offices, roomy brownstones, cramped, over-priced apartments. Jeremiah heard from them occasionally, phone ringing early in the morning or late at night, some woman he used to wake up with or some man he used to go to the gym with calling, tears like something obscene lodged in the throat, waiting for him to tell them he was fine. That never happened, no good news, the best he could do was tell them not to worry, not to come by, don't feel guilty, no-body's fault.

Jeremiah was all the time playing therapist like he didn't need two hour-long sessions with his own therapist to get through the week without hating himself, circumstance, beautiful New York women who languidly wrapped long legs about his waist. His therapist was a woman, brown and round and short. Her hair was in long locks down her back, perfume subtle. On her ears, wrist, and fingers, gold shone like her body a magnet for sun and stars. Dr. Jones was a wife and mother and grandmother and he leaned on her because her arms always spread wide, her lap large enough for him, big old grown man, to climb in, curl up. She had offices in Brooklyn and Monday and Thursday morning he made the trip, his body tired and worn out, umbrella shiny wet with never-ending rain, feet dragging all along Flatbush Avenue. Dr. Jones's office was in a converted brownstone, decorated like a well-tended home. Comfortable couches, large, bright red pillows thrown about the floor, books placed haphazardly, without any kind of order, on polished pine shelves. Her subtle lavender perfume all throughout the office and he loved the smell. It reminded him of summers as a child and the lavender that grew all over Eden, grew wild and ferocious and everything, everyone covered with sweet scent.

Their appointments always began the same. She came from behind her desk, barefoot, stocking feet striding across worn carpet, kissed him lightly on the cheek, stepped back, looked him hard up and down.

"How you doing today, baby?"

He would have traveled for miles, walked through piles of snow and slush, even shit, to hear a woman call him baby again.

"I'm hanging in there, Dr. Jones."

She sat back down behind her desk and he settled down on comfortable sofa, muted beige cushions cradling his weight, all the support that he needed.

"Good. No reason to give up the good fight. Never no reason for that."

He'd thought about it, thought about giving up and letting it all go. His body young and fresh again, his mind free from the weight of when over, when done, when absolutely and inevitably no more. He got scared lying in bed sometimes, scared with the covers over him like a warm cocoon, scared when he considered what came after, if anything. He tried hard not to become preoccupied with dying things. Bees missing one wing, ants carelessly crushed strolling busy streets, dying snails baking on cement, moths who flew into the light at the top of his apartment steps and burned bright like sun hurting eyes on hot summer days, made him completely numb—mouth hanging partway open and drool running from the corners. The rest of his life just a waiting game to see if there was anything else out there that could make drool roll from the corners of his mouth and leave no tears just sand running from dry and burning eyes.

"Dr. Jones, I don't know how much fight I got left."

"Enough. Don't you worry about it. We all have just enough."

He looked forward to his visits, looked forward to walking into her warm office, smelling her lavender perfume, feeling her lips, cool and soft and stained deep red, against his face. She wasn't afraid to touch him, didn't keep wiping hands down clothes like she was afraid to get what he had, didn't try to discreetly run to the bathroom to wash hands and do an all-around-body check every fifteen minutes. In her office it was easy not to think about holding his breath and diving into earth, scooting his body around like fishes stuck drying out on sandy beaches, worms crawling in his hair and beneath his clothes.

Dr. Jones sat forward on her desk, placed her beautifully round head in the palms of her hands, gave a wide smile.

"Anything come up you'd like to start with?"

He looked all around the room, down at his own hands, hands almost unrecognizable he had lost so much weight.

"No, well, there's still me and my father."

"Okay. How's that going?"

"It's just us here, really. He's been taking care of me,

bringing me dinner, making sure I have everything I need. He's all I have right now. But there's all this, I don't know, all this awkwardness like we sort of circling around each other. I want to say something to him but he's been really good about it all, you know?"

"How was he supposed to be?"

"What do you mean?"

"You said, 'he's been really good with it.' How did you think he was going to be?"

"I don't know. It's not that I expected him to disown me or anything like that. I just don't want him to feel uncomfortable because when he's uncomfortable I'm uncomfortable."

"Okay. What are some of the things you'd like to say to him?"

"I want to tell him not to worry about it but . . . I'm his child. His child. I know he can look at me and see there's a whole hell of a lot to worry about."

"Why shouldn't he worry? Why shouldn't he be concerned?"

"Look, it's hard enough for me to even process what I'm feeling, hard enough for me just to get out of bed in the morning. I don't want to have to deal with his hurt as well. I got enough hurt to last me until."

"Until when?"

"Just until. It's an expression. You never heard it before?"

"No, I don't think so."

"Well anyway, I don't want him to go through this by himself. It's too much."

"What about you? How do you want to go through this?"

"I've been thinking I don't want to be here, not when it's all said and done."

"Where're you trying to be?"

"Home. I want to go home."

"From what you've told me, you had good reasons for leaving Eden."

Jeremiah had forgotten that he had told her what he, Aspasia, and Hawk Eye had found in Eden as children. As children they were inseparable, where one went the other two faithfully followed. He was closer to them than both his brothers until they realized what they had, by sheer accident, discovered. Discovered in a town where they knew everyone and the front doors of homes left carelessly open during the day. Found in a place where their parents told them each night before they put them to bed that there were no bad people, that there was nothing to fear other than monsters under the bed and hiding in closets. He learned, with Aspasia and Hawk Eye, that terror didn't respect Eden's borders at all. It left them all fragmented, changed their friendships, made them all start looking for ways to get out. Jeremiah left for New York as soon as he turned eighteen. Aspasia slept around, traveled distances with other men until she realized all roads led her to Pete. Hawk Eye stopped caring about life altogether, spent his time running in front of speeding cars.

"I did, but it's still home. There's no way to get around that. I wake up thinking about Eden, go to sleep with the candy-sweet smell of Eden on my tongue."

"You think things changed there?

"I don't know. I just know . . . I just feel that Eden is where I need to be. And I want to see my mother before . . . I want to see my mother."

"Okay. Home sounds good to me."

He left Dr. Jones's office, rain still falling, umbrella still shiny and wet, body still tired and worn but smiling, a lightness in his step.

Daddy helped him pack his bags and close up the apartment. He wasn't coming back. Daddy drove him to Port Authority and waited in line with him until the Greyhound bus began boarding. Daddy stood guard over him like he was a small child bound for first summer away at a distant overnight camp.

"You got everything you need? All your medicines?"

"Daddy, I got everything."

"You sure, now? You don't want to do a final check just in case?"

They did a final check, bending down in the Greyhound bus line, his pills in their tightly capped plastic bottles jingling like coins in the bottoms of old ladies purses. People in front and behind trying to read the prescriptions on the bottles, his hands damp with sweat, wondering if, after seeing all those bottles and bottles of pills, anyone would be brave enough to sit next to him.

Daddy waited with him until the line began moving and then he stepped away, stepped away with a final kiss on the forehead, Daddy's arms heavy and tender around his shoulders.

"You have a safe trip."

"I will."

"I'll come when . . . Just you don't worry. I'll come."

"I know you will."

"Love you, boy."

"Love you too, Daddy."

Daddy walked away through the crowd, all these people coming and going and going and coming, his steps slow and hesitant like his age finally caught up and jumped on his back after years and years. He wondered if Daddy was as tired as he was of long, continuous goodbye. A good-bye that lasted for weeks and months and who knew how much longer, how often and fast and quietly a heart could weep.

The Greyhound bus pulled out onto slick, tar, city streets, rain lightly tapping feet against the windows and hood of the bus. The bus a little more than half full, mostly teenagers and women, and smelled unpleasantly of unknown, unwashed bodies. Teenagers dressed in jeans and shirts and shell-topped Addidases, earphones on and Walkmans resting in their laps, heads nodding. Run-DMC's album *Raising Hell* a steady drone from earphones, quieting the hum of the air conditioner. There was a young girl in front of him popping her gum in tune with the beat, hands splayed out on the headrest, hair in an asymmetrical cut, long nails painted bright bloodred. Where was she going with nails like that? She couldn't be more than fifteen and nails like a woman going to meet a man somewhere.

The rain followed them out of New York and onto the highway. He kept checking highway markers, told rain that by the next exit it had to stop, calm down, show some self-control. Rain just kept coming, sometimes hard and sometimes soft but always coming. When he had talked to Pete he found out that Eden was in the middle of a heat wave and he was waiting to get off the bus and see nothing but big old sun in clear blue skies, waiting to feel lash of heat all over his skin.

Summers in Eden were the best time when he was a child. No school and days so long they stretched out into years. He ran up and down the streets, played tag and green light–red light and hide and seek with Hawk Eye and Aspasia. Sometimes Pete played with them if he wasn't busy with his own friends. Quincy was too mean to do anything but hang out with the rest of the hoodlums in town. They had walked down to the convenience store to buy ice-cold pops, so cold the bottle sweating and sticky sweet pop left a headache going down. Cats licked themselves in summer, fur sticky with children's Popsicles dripped into the street. Popsicles and grape soda, hard Now and Later candy and watermelon bubblegum matted in fur, smooth white cat skin showing between winding and uneven parts.

July 4 was one big party on Lake Erie, everyone brought packed-full coolers of cold cuts and hugs and beer and wine coolers. Grills were dragged into the park area surrounding the lake, people spread out colorful tablecloths across old wooden park tables, spread faded, well-used blankets beneath trees. Children ran wild, swam in the lake, rolled in the grass, staunchly ignored bug bites and scrapes and bruises, Fourth of July no time for the faint of heart. The day ended in firework displays, fireworks filling the sky like millions and millions of brightly colored falling stars, explosion upon explosion. The Fourth right around the corner, he was going to hold on to see all that brilliance, be greedy enough to enjoy all that good time.

School out now and he still remembered the horror of Eden High, the only thing to do in town on Friday nights was go to the high school football or basketball games or get drunk and high in someone's basement. High school football and basketball players big news, excluding the obituaries, in the daily paper—how many first downs and how many receptions and how many baskets and how many steals. They strolled the ugliness of gleaming high school hallways with polished tiled floors like sports the only thing worth doing in a town where Burger King was the only club for people under eighteen to hang out. High school girls spent hours on nails and hair and makeup, bought every teenage magazine available for soft skin and white teeth and fruit smelling breath. Homecoming queen was a superstar walking the streets long after homecoming over and done like her cape still trailed after her and her crown still sat any old way on her carefully curled and done head.

The rain followed him down the highway, happy, care-free companion, clouds in the sky and sky black and muddy. He gazed out the window as scenery passed, like watching a moving picture. An hour on the bus and they were out of New York, somewhere in Pennsylvania. There were trees, an abundance of trees with soft looking, new green leaves of spring even though it was early summer. There was grass, grass that stretched as far as the eye could see, grass that went on forever, eventually bored him with its tenacity and predictability. There were fields, fields of corn or wheat, or some other crop. He couldn't tell the difference. Crops aligned perfectly, crops withered from poor maintenance and bad conditions, crops shooting from the earth, healthy and menacing, crops that bent and swayed and wept with wind and rain.

There were mountains, impressive and invulnerable, mountains in shades or browns and reds and grays, moun-tains of rock, of dirt, mountains with trees scattered along their sides. The highway rolled by beneath huge black tires that effortlessly ate up the distance. Dead animals along the road; soft, furry small things with blood and flesh spread out underneath like bright silk scarves. Reminded him of dead cats in the middle of streets of small blocks in Brook-lyn. Cats with glazed or closed eyes, skin spread almost from pavement to pavement, matted and wet with death. The Greyhound bus had all windows up and air condition-ing on. The dark highway was separated by sheets of tinted glass. Tinted glass kept the smell of dead things and rocks and stunted trees out of aisles and seats smelling like stale cigarettes, bodies, and breath.

He thought of women, women hanging like a dull moon from the sky, women shooting up from the black and moist earth like crops, women falling from trees like dead leaves. Women always at his back and always at his front, cutting him in two, their nails bloodred like the girl's in front of him. His life nothing but women from Mama and all the old women in Eden, to beautiful New York women trying to walk like they had all they needed and limping through the streets of Brooklyn and Manhattan. He chased them down, down Brooklyn blocks with B-boys break dancing on spread out cardboard, hands and arms and feet and heads performing amazing feats of gravity, chased them down in Manhattan boutiques where clothes and shoes ridiculously expensive.

They wanted to be chased, be caught, wanted arms around them in the middle of the night when all the things they did or all the things they owned were simply not enough. He knew about not enough, watched Mama, when Daddy still living with them but acting like a child, walk year round with arms wrapped tight about her small body. Mama with sweaters always thrown over her shoulders, heavy quilts always on the bed trying to keep herself warm.

He didn't think he ever took advantage, ever used that desperate need draped around beautiful bodies, clinging to brown butternut skin like overpowering perfume, making gorgeous full heads of hair fall out. He had a mama. He tried to be kind, tried to avoid lies, false promises, angry words barreling like prizefighter hands.

Dozens and dozens of women played in the dark behind closed eyelids. Women with full, round bodies, women slender with no hips and ass, women with hair pulled back tight in a professional bun or left loose to frame the face, women with smiling eyes and laughing mouths or eyes all the time wet and mouths all the time pouting. They danced in the dark behind closed eyes, formed a kind of soul-train line, women clapping hands and stomping feet on the side, twisting and strutting down the middle. No music in his head, just women dancing and dancing like they had no worries, nothing to do but keep on keeping on. All their names still familiar, still comfortable on his tongue. He never forgot the name of someone he took to bed, his skin and breath and heart collecting and burning beneath the weight of all those names, all those memories. Shanise and Jasmine and Nicole and Whitney and Aliyah and Sarah and Naja and on and on, memories of soft bodies and damp skin and brief pleasure.

Thing that hurt him most now, how brief the pleasure, how fleeting. The easy fall into sleep next to a warm, wet body hoping for her, for himself that something more would come out of it, the ever elusive long term I-will-put-up-with-your-shit-indefinitely relationship. Everyone was looking for the next best thing. It was hard to be happy with any-one when eyes were already roaming, thoughts already sprinting ahead to someone somewhere better.

He was never any woman's good enough.

Long nights and lazy afternoons spent with different women. Brown bodies moved like racing wildfire across damp sheets, got rug burns on carpeted floors, used chairs and sofas to anchor and hold position. He was so greedy for all that pretty brown, gold, red, black flesh, so greedy for warmth and smiles and sighs and secrets told in the middle of the night and conveniently forgotten in the morning. He knew better, knew from all those years in church with Mama and his brothers, all those mornings in Sunday school that gluttony a sin. Almost like bright lights and frighteningly tall skyscrapers of New York City drugged him, like New York with all its diversity and music and magic the same as crack inhaled deep from the pipe. He knew nothing on earth more mysterious, more uncompromisingly beautiful than breasts that flared into waists and waists that flared into asses and asses that flared into hips and thighs, all that hidden poetry.

He called them all, beautiful New York City women, when test results in and no way to avoid weekly appointments and therapists and a medicine cabinet full of brightly colored pills in dull brown plastic jars. Plastic jars with safety caps, caps he sometimes couldn't open because that's how absolutely safe they were and for him there was no more safety, no waiting things out. Some women hung up on him in shock, some women raged, called him everything but a child of God, some women cried softly into the phone, told him he was going to be fine.

He was left wondering, as if it made any kind of difference, who? Whose touch, whose uncompromisingly beautiful woman's flesh left him rotting inside?

Chapter Twelve

Women usually started coming over around ten in the morning Monday through Friday, sometimes earlier, sometimes later. Women from across the street or a few houses down with slippers still on their feet and loose, comfortable clothing hanging from their bodies like silk and lace. Women with hair still braided or tied down from the night before, women with big, round curlers scattered throughout the head like a schoolgirl's colorful barrettes. Aspasia put Lula in the playpen or spread a blanket out on the floor with all her toys. Lula loved teddy bears and dolls with wide eyes, fed dolls and bears make-believe food from plastic, child-sized bowls and plates; shoved bottles filled with make-believe juice and milk down their throats.

Aspasia got her sewing machine ready in the dining room. It was an old sewing machine, sturdy and heavy, in her family for years and years, belonged to Mama and Grandma, each and every woman with her blood. Eliza didn't have time for piecing together fabric, creating patterns, feeling light silk or soft cotton rub against the skin, fabric like kisses along the backs of her hands and lower arms. Eliza helped people and she kept them clothed. Loved making dresses and pants and blouses for women, loved making pretty party dresses for first birthdays and last birthdays and anniversaries and christenings. Dining room bright, painted warm, golden yellow with high ceilings and shining hardwood floors. It doubled as her workspace because the room the most beautiful in the house, the place she felt the most comfortable. Dark cherry wooden beams crossed the ceiling similar to beams in old, historic churches. The fireplace, the centerpiece of the room, was made from same cherry dark wood. Detailed designs framed the fireplace and mantel, created an illusion of comfort and wealth. The house, particularly the dining room, a testament to craftsmanship, built solely by black hands in the late 1800s when houses built to last.

She carefully laid out materials and scissors on the dinning room table where Lula's quick and busy hands couldn't reach them. Lula sat on her blanket in the center of the floor, rolled about like a puppy, hummed a tuneless song, played absently with her feet and toes.

Ms. Pat from across the street strolled in without knocking.

"Aspasia, honey? Where you and Lula at?"

Aspasia smelled Ms. Pat's rosewater; Ms. Pat always made grand entrances and smelled like whole gardens of roses.

"We in here in the dining room, Ms. Pat."

Ms. Pat was a small, slim woman in her early fifties, dyed blond hair cropped close to the head, always drenched in rose or lavender water. Ms. Pat one of the women who opened their door for Sunday dinners and offered advice and hugs and kisses after Mama passed. Aspasia and Eliza raised by just about every woman in town, got pieces of what they needed to be grown in the world from a bunch of loving hands. Some taught them how to cook, how to stand at the stove and tell when food good and done, how to set a table and serve food with love, fill stomachs of family and friends with kindness. Some taught them how to clean house, clean a little bit each day so that cleaning never overwhelmed and the house never in total disarray—dust on hardwood floors, clothes piled on dressers, junk scattered from basement to bedrooms. Some taught them how to be comfortable in their own skin, how to love their nappy hair and round ass and thighs, enjoy their bodies, play to their strengths, learn from their weaknesses.

Ms. Pat Aspasia's favorite because she did just exactly what pleased her. Some days got dressed and some days sat out on the porch in housecoat until the sun no longer in the sky. Nobody had the nerve to tell her to go put some clothes on. Ms. Pat in housecoat and slippers sipped at cool iced tea in a sweating glass like she was all done up and decked out waiting for some man to come calling.

Ms. Pat kissed Aspasia on the cheek, close to the mouth. Aspasia felt the stain of Ms. Pat's red lipstick against her skin.

"How you doing, Ms. Pat?"

"Fine, honey girl. Just fine."

Ms. Pat surprised Lula on the floor and the baby stopped, startled, laughed. Ms. Pat lifted her high over her head, Lula grabbed frantically for her tinted glasses.

"There she is. There's my pretty baby."

Lula so excited spit rushing from her mouth, down her chin, between the baby fat folds of her neck, onto Ms. Pat's face.

Ms. Pat put her down, Lula fussed a bit and Ms. Pat did an old two-step, playing the clown.

"Enough of that now. You got to learn to keep that spit from getting people if you want to be entertained at close range."

Lula went back to crawling around her blanket, picking up and throwing down toys, sucking absently at fingers and toes.

Ms. Pat sat down in bright red cushioned chair in front of the gated-off fireplace like she had walked for miles and not just down the street, fanning herself, sweat rolling slow from her blond head.

"You feeling okay, Ms. Pat?"

"Hot. Baby girl, I'm hot."

Aspasia nodded and unfolded the dress she was working on for Ms. Pat. The final fitting was the only reason Ms. Pat left the comfort of her house, the coolness of her shaded porch, braved relentless heat. The dress dark blue with streaks of lavender, breezy thin-strapped summer dress that fell gently and still managed to hug the hips. Aspasia made most of Ms. Pat's clothes. When she first started out Ms. Pat strutted slow around town like one of those runway models, free advertisement.

"The heat has to break. I can't recall no summer like this and we haven't hit July yet."

Eliza came through the front door, she knew it was Eliza because Eliza danced instead of walked, loose skirts giggled at her ankles and calves, hips swayed in easy rhythm, arms at her sides. When Eliza rushed, she favored the stylized dances of the seventies when women and men danced with cigarettes in their mouths, posed with hands on hips. When Eliza took her time she was a slow drag, sweet and coy, feet moving instinctually in the dark.

"Aspasia?"

"We in here, Eliza."

Eliza danced in the room, hands and arms filled with brown paper bags.

"I brought you some things for Lula's teething. Made you some tea to help mellow you out and . . ."

Ms. Pat interrupted her.

"Eliza, I know you've got better manners than to come into a room and not speak."

Eliza laughed.

"Ms. Pat, I didn't even see you there, you being so quiet and all."

"So?"

Eliza went to Ms. Pat, kissed her soft, wrinkled forehead.

"So, hello. How you feeling? Arthritis still messing with you?"

Ms. Pat rubbed absently at her hand, hand so stiff sometimes it hung dead and useless from her wrist.

"I could use more of whatever it was you gave me before. I'm running out."

"I'll make you some more salve, bring it by this afternoon."

Ms. Pat scolded Aspasia gently for paying more attention to fabric on the table than people.

"Stop messing with all that stuff and get me something cool to drink."

"I'm sorry, Ms. Pat. I was going to offer but you didn't give me a chance."

"Taking too long, can't you see I'm just about ready to die? Aspasia, what that baby got in her mouth?"

Ms. Pat got on the floor with Lula, gently pried her mouth open. Lula was furious and trying to bite.

"Now you bite me, I'm going to bite you back."

Lula must have taken the threat seriously because she

calmed down and let Ms. Pat pull soggy paper from her mouth.

Eliza took Lula from Ms. Pat, placed Lula on her hip, Lula's short, fat baby legs wrapped comfortable around her. She whispered nonsense in Lula's ears, growled in baby-soft tender folds of Lula's chin and neck. Lula laughed.

"Aspasia, can you get me something to drink as well?'

Aspasia headed for the kitchen.

"Ms. Pat, lemonade all right?"

"Lemonade just fine."

Aspasia called to Eliza.

"What about you, baby?"

"I can do lemonade."

The kitchen shiny with morning sun and already heat thick in the room because no air conditioners downstairs, only upstairs in their bedrooms. Aspasia could hear Ms. Pat and Eliza talking to Lula like she had good sense, not talking like she was a pet, some kind of cat or dog. Lula was treated like an actual person and Lula talked back, having a conversation, waiting patiently for Ms. Pat's or Eliza's voice to pause before she responded.

Eliza was blood of her blood and flesh of her flesh, sister and surrogate mama, dependable and most of the time kind. They were closer than most sisters; murder between them a bond like steel beams supporting towering skyscrapers in New York or Chicago skylines.

The refrigerator worked hard, humming loudly in the quiet. Light blue walls of the kitchen like looking up into the sky outside. The tiled floors comfortable beneath her feet, not yet reflecting the heat from glare of the sun coming in through kitchen windows. Kitchen was clean because Pete had washed dishes and put everything back in its proper place after he cooked breakfast for him and Lula.

One of the things she loved best about Pete—he cleaned. Living with Daddy she and Eliza were sometimes no better than maids. Daddy was a general who gave out orders and directions without hugs or kisses or smiles, no kind of affection at all. Eliza did the majority of the work, always telling her to go play, go do something because she had her entire life to mop floors and wash clothes.

She and Eliza never talked about murder, man dead and buried in the cemetery at the edge of town because of them. The enormity of taking a life was almost too sacred for words, nothing at all to do but let the dead stay buried.

Aspasia emptied ice into glasses, poured cold lemonade from the refrigerator. Thought about being thirteen, a child, with brother Carl waiting and watching her on the way to and from school, to and from the convenience store. He was always there, smiling at her, his smile told her all the things he wanted to do to her, all the things he wanted her to do to him. Sometimes he called out to her, when the street empty and no one paying attention. His voice hammers slamming into her chest, his voice rough hands holding her down and forcing apart her thighs.

She didn't say a word to Eliza. Eliza stunned and heart-broken and raging, the thought of brother Carl enough to send her into fits and when Eliza had fits the flowers died, the herbs and the vegetables refused to grow, bright daytime sky in Eden turned dark and solemn overhead.

She avoided him, sidestepped his stares, ignored his voice trailing behind her, trying to sneak up under her skirts, unfasten shirts, pull down jeans and shorts. He finally caught her and if she hadn't been thirteen, a child, she would have known that he wasn't really scared of Eliza or teasing the way boys in school sometimes pulled at her hair and grabbed, with no real enthusiasm, at her ass.

Eliza sent her to the convenience store for oil to fry chicken; she was walking home, oil in brown paper bag, light in her hands, when he fell in step beside her. She kept her eyes straight ahead, forced her skinny, long child legs to move fast over concrete, looked frantically for other people, but it was near dinnertime and no one in the streets, people comfortable in homes.

"How you doing, baby girl?"

His voice thick and slurred, he wasn't drunk, no alcohol on his breath. He was completely sober, completely in his right mind. Blood rushed through her body, pulse drummed at her neck, hands damp and clenched about the bottle of oil, in the crumbled brown paper bag.

He moved closer, hip bumping hers, hand insistent at her lower back, rubbing and squeezing never before touched flesh.

"I said how you doing, baby girl?"

His hand at her waist hardened, held her still, slowly turned her to face him. The oil fell from her numb fingers. The plastic round bottle in brown paper bag rolled down the sidewalk, into the gutter, filth.

His face was in her neck, his lips and tongue and teeth on her. His hands were on her ass, moving up and up and up over her belly to her breasts and she couldn't breathe, cried hard and silent, body pitched and rocked with sobs and the force of his hips rolling against her.

He kept her there—left marks on her neck and chin and cheeks, bruises at her lips and breasts and waist—until he heard people coming toward them, heard women laughing and talking loud.

He pulled away, picked up the oil from the gutter, forced the oil into her hands, wiped tenderly at her tears, her bruised mouth.

"See you around, baby girl. Oh, yes I will."

Aspasia ran all the way home, feet unsteady and stumbling, eating up sidewalk. She ran through the kitchen door, startled Eliza at the counter mashing boiled potatoes for their dinner.

Eliza turned around quick, smiled puzzled.

"Aspasia, what took you so long?"

Legs gave out beneath her, the weight of her body too much. She collapsed on kitchen floor, tile cool and pleasant against her cheeks.

Eliza sat down next to Aspasia, put her head in her lap, stroked her hair over and over.

"Tell me what happened, Aspasia."

Eliza's voice was calm and patient, waiting and it all came out. Brother Carl following her and brother Carl putting hands on her and leaving marks on her flesh, marks festering beneath the skin for the rest of her life.

Eliza made her sit up.

"Let me look at you."

Bruises on her face were flaring and colorful, her lips swollen and her eyes dull and red and wet with tears.

Eliza kissed her mouth, her cheeks, her wet eyes.

"He must be a fool. He must be because I told him I'd kill him."

Aspasia's eyes widened, anxiety arched her spine.

"Don't, Eliza, don't worry about it. It's not that bad."

"Hush now, baby. Let me put you in the tub. None of this is your fault, none of it because of anything you did or didn't do."

Eliza took her upstairs, ran water for her bath, put in fresh lavender and rose petals from her garden in the bath water. Eliza helped her bathe, helped hot water and lavender and rose petals wash her clean inside and out. Wrapped her in thick soft towel, made her tea to help her sleep, laid down in bed with her, rocked her like she used to when Aspasia was younger and Mama just dead.

"You stay with me, Eliza."

"Of course, I'm going to stay with you. Go to sleep."

Aspasia startled and scared in the middle of the night, sat up in bed, searched for Eliza but Eliza was gone, nowhere in the house and the moon low and lonely in nighttime sky. The next morning brother Carl found dead, lifeless body swaying gently from the rafters in his mama's basement.

Aspasia went back to the dining room with Ms. Pat's and Eliza's lemonade. Eliza drank her lemonade down quick, in a rush to get out the door.

"I've got to go, Aspasia. I'll call you later. Ms. Pat, I'll bring that by for you this afternoon."

Aspasia held up a hand before Eliza danced by her.

"Wait a minute. Jeremiah's coming home."

"When will he be here?"

"Tomorrow morning."

"What you need me to do, Aspasia?"

"Oh, baby. Whatever you can."

Eliza blew kisses at Lula, Lula rolled and jumped trying to catch them all, and Eliza danced out the front door, skirts still giggling against her ankles and calves. Ms. Pat got up from Lula and the floor slowly and for the first time Aspasia realized she was old, long past retirement, hands and face baby soft like Lula's skin, the way the skin of old folks took on the brightness of childhood.

"You'll be done today, Aspasia?"

"I think so. One more fitting and we'll take it from there."

"How is Jeremiah doing?"

"Ms. Pat, he's doing. That's about all I can say."

"He was a wonderful child. You know I talk to his mama, and her heart is just broken."

"He's still wonderful. And we all got broken hearts, Ms. Pat. Broken some way or another."

"I'll say amen to that."

"Me too, Ms. Pat."

"You got music, Aspasia? Something to listen to while we get this thing done?"

She had a collection of blues and jazz and gospel tapes. Pete liked soul and rhythm and blues. She liked Billy Holiday and Bessie Smith and Mahalia Jackson.

"What you feel like today, Ms. Pat?"

"Let me think a minute, now. I woke up this morning thinking it was Sunday, just all ready to go to church. Put Mahalia on."

Music was all through the house like the smell of Ms. Pat's rosewater. Mahalia's deep, fine voice cooled off the house, beat back the heat trying to sneak in from outside. She had to finish Ms. Pat within the hour because she had at least three more women coming over definitely and two who might if they could get away from work and kids early. Aspasia was busy from ten in the morning to around six in the evening. She stopped midday to give Lula lunch, sponge her small, brown body, and put her down for a nap. Nap time Aspasia's favorite part of the day, Lula smiling at her with her four front teeth from her crib, blowing kisses and pulling at her braids to put herself to sleep. All her braids were messed and unraveled over her head when she woke up.

Ms. Pat was happy to wait on her dress and play with Lula. Ms. Pat's daughter, Lee, lived down in Chicago, she rarely got to see or hold her grandbabies. Lula was delighted with Ms. Pat. Lula well taken care of and well loved, capable of amazing feats each and every hour. Lula, with her smiles and crying and grasping, made Aspasia think of Mama. Her mama, Eliza Queen Todd. Aspasia loved Mama's name, loved the fact that Mama was a queen. Mama told her a long time ago on the beaches of Lake Erie that sometimes love just wasn't enough. She was learning now with Pete and Lula what Mama had forgot to mention, that sometimes love was too much, hoarded at all costs until it turned sour and rotten.

Chapter Thirteen

The shadows beneath giant old tree in the front yard were deeper and fuller, but it was not quite night when Red Cap pulled up in the driveway. Pete sat a minute, trying to will aching, tired bones well. His clothes dirty, boots covered in construction-site filth, and the dry taste of cement in his mouth. Nothing cooled down, heat just being blown about by hot breezes. Children sat exhausted with glazed eyes on porches all up and down the block. Brown boys plucking absently at their shoelaces, swatting lazy at mosquitoes; brown girls tugging slowly at long pig tails, popping gum and blowing bubbles.

The pop of gum like little firecrackers on July 4 all up and down the street. July 4 sneaking up on them. It was already the middle of June and the grill had to be dragged out the shed and cleaned, rose bushes pruned in the backyard, yard chairs and tables sat out so Aspasia and the baby had someplace nice to sit on cool days after all the heat broke. Jeremiah's room had to be aired out and sheets changed on the bed because Jeremiah on his way home.

Last time he saw Jeremiah was two years ago when Jeremiah came for Mama's wedding to Red. Red was carrying on like his wedding the first wedding in all creation and in the middle of things to be done, suits to try on, finding strippers for Red's bachelor party, and getting the house set up for the reception, there wasn't any time at all for them to talk.

Pete had cornered Jeremiah after the wedding, stared at Jeremiah's healthy brown face, noticed all the weight that he put on, how his smile came easy.

"You all right?"

Jeremiah hugged him hard, laughed. "I'm fine man, I'm fine."

Jeremiah was coming home and Pete wanted to see that same, smooth, glowing skin, hear that same absent laugh. Pete gathered his lunch pail from the floor of Red's truck. The Temptations wailed about "My Girl" from the house, and the Temptations "My Girl" like a welcome mat at his feet.

"Okay, Red. See you tomorrow."

"Give my Lula a kiss."

Red drove recklessly down the street knowing the whole neighborhood, streets included, nothing more than a giant playground for children. No danger at all tonight of kids rushing from between parked cars, stumbling blindly after racing, bouncing balls, playing double-dutch in the middle of the road. All the children were absolutely wiped out.

Sharon from next door was in the dining room with Lula on her hip, staring, eyes narrowed, over Aspasia's shoulder. Aspasia was at the sewing machine, fixing something on some gauzy, pretty thing, muted yellow and made to fall over a woman's skin, all the creases and folds like mystery or bodies touching in the middle of the night.

Lula pulled away from Sharon, screaming "Da! Da!"

Her voice shrill and loud enough to drown out "My Girl," loud enough for Sharon to put her down in a hurry, get all that noise away from her ears.

Lula walked to him, no hesitancy at all. Lula had been walking since about nine months. Now walking forward was no longer a challenge and she was constantly trying to walk backward, tripping over her own feet and hard toys and soft pillows left on the floor. He picked her up, little legs wrapped immediately around his waist, little arms holding tight to his neck. Lula didn't care about the musky, borderline offensive smell riding his skin, didn't care about dirt caked onto his clothes.

Pete settled her on his hip, bounced her lightly and ate at baby fat cheeks. "Here's my girl, here's my baby . . ."

Lula laughed and laughed and Aspasia looked up, smiled at them both.

"Give me a second Pete, I'll be done with Sharon in a minute."

Pete didn't want to sit down, didn't want to touch anything or move too much at all, dirty as he was.

"Take your time. How you doing, Sharon?"

Sharon had long, permed and curled hair. She was yellow, her yellow skin hinting at red like she was always just a minute from blushing. Sharon was middle school princess and High School homecoming queen, pretty, pretty woman. Men chased her from one end of town to the next, and fell over all her crowns. Their hands stained red, purple, light pink, black from all the makeup that she wore. She settled on Vernon, plain looking, plain speaking and kind. She went away to Howard University down in D.C., where she got homecoming queen two years in a row before coming back home. Biggest disappointment her mama and daddy ever suffered was watching their child get off the Greyhound bus in the middle of town not to visit but to stay for good—all for some nappy-head boy who worked with his hands, did construction that didn't require any kind of education at all.

"Same old same old, Pete."

"Why you getting all pretty?"

"Anniversary coming up. Four years. Mama and Daddy throwing us a party, it's just about killing them. Don't tell me you all didn't get the invitation? Party's tomorrow night."

Aspasia laughed.

"Look at you getting all fancy, sending mail. Ms. College."

"Aspasia, stop playing. You got the invitation didn't you?"

Aspasia laughed harder. "Of course we did. We'll be there. Jeremiah coming home tomorrow, so I'm sure he'll be there, too. See, that's what happens when you go off to fancy colleges and start using the post office."

"I'd love to see Jeremiah, really I would. And college didn't do me a bit of good. No jobs anyway but the Sweet Cake factory. And you can say what you want, but it's too damn hot to be going door to door for some invitations."

Lula licked at the dirty skin of his forearm and Pete put her down.

"Let me get in the shower before Lula eats all the dirt off me. See you, Sharon."

"Hey, Pete? You think Vernon home yet?"

"Nope. He was still at the site when I left."

Shower sprayed luke warm water and he adjusted the knobs, the temperature closer to cool. Pete watched dirt from his skin go in dark spirals down the drain. He braced his hands against the wall, put his head under water falling hard. Lining the shower were fruit-and flower-scented glycerin soaps, herbal shampoos, shaving creams, and razors. Pete didn't really care how he smelled, not one of those men who woke up in the mornings and went out in the evenings slathered down in cologne. Pete grabbed the bar of soap closest to him. Vanilla rose from the rich, white lather.

Summer days so long and the heat made days go on and on, made nights uncomfortable and far too short. Never enough rest and Pete tried to figure out when exhaustion settled into bones to stay awhile. Maybe right after Lula's birth when Aspasia was still sore, healing, walking around cradling her insides with one hand and Lula with the other, dazed. He came home sometimes and both Lula and Aspasia were crying or Lula screaming and Aspasia pacing frantically across the floor.

Lula had the worst colic he'd ever seen and nothing to do but wait it out, no way at all to comfort her. They tried hot baths, tried laying her skin against skin, heartbeat to heartbeat; they walked hallways, up and down and up and down stairs, traded her back and forth between them. Overwhelming love and overwhelming fear that Lula just might cry herself into some kind of coma kept feet moving. They just stumbled about sometimes with eyes closed. Eliza made all kinds of salves and tinctures and steam inhalations but nothing worked and she finally gave up, convinced that Lula just liked the sound of her own voice. The colic lasted just over three whole months. The first night Lula slept soundly they checked on her every fifteen minutes, positive that she wasn't breathing, her neck caught some kind of way between the spaces of the crib.

Those first three months were hell, but seemed like nothing at all when he realized that he had somehow been duped into a never-ending job. Before Lula was actually in the world, existing outside of Aspasia's belly, he figured he'd serve eighteen years. Eighteen good years being attentive, teaching right from wrong, being loving and fair, spanking only when left with no other alternative.

Pete rinsed white vanilla lather from his body, turned off the shower, stepped out into the hallway, and hollered down the stairs.

"Aspasia? Sharon still here?"

Aspasia's voice was muffled from the kitchen.

"Nope. She just left."

Heat demanded boxers and a light T-shirt. He went downstairs, bright hardwood floors cool against bare feet. The dining room cleaned, bare of untouched, neatly stacked fabric, Lula's toys all put away, Aspasia's sewing machine pushed back against the wall. Aspasia and Lula were in the kitchen. Lula sat in her high chair, happily banging plastic spoons and a bowl. Aspasia made plates at the counter.

"You hungry?"

She smiled, turned slightly toward him, dimples deepening, hair nappy and pretty on top her head, sweet line of sweat gathered between her breasts.

"Starving. What you cook?"

Lula still banged and Pete was always amazed at how much noise one child, just barely a toddler, could make, and how easy it was to ignore day in and day out.

"I fried some chicken, made a pasta salad."

Pete took Lula's bowl. Lula screamed briefly in protest and went back to banging. At the counter he pulled pieces of chicken away from the bone, cut up slices of pasta and vegetables for Lula.

"We could of done sandwiches. I hate to think of you at the stove in all this heat."

Aspasia laughed, bumped her hip against his.

"We did sandwiches last night and the night before and the night before. I was all sandwiched out, had a taste for fried chicken."

"All right. But don't think you need to cook. I'm okay with sandwiches and Lula eats anything you put on her plate. I'm driving tomorrow, I'll stop and get some barbeque on the way home."

Aspasia put plates on the table and Pete gave Lula her bowl and pulled her high chair close to his seat so he could help feed her. Aspasia picked at her chicken with fingers, peeling off all the crisp skin and saving it for last, the best part.

"How many women came through today?"

"About fifteen. Some for fittings, some to show me what they want."

"You need to open a shop."

"It wouldn't work. Women, especially older women, the main ones who prefer to have their clothes made, rather come to the house. Seems more like a social visit and they're happy to help me with Lula besides."

Pete watched close while Lula struggled to get down a piece of chicken, mouth and jaw working.

Aspasia rubbed a cold beer bottle against her neck and he watched the trail of wet left behind on her brown, bright skin.

"Okay. What happened today?"

Aspasia leaned closer to him across the table, large black eyes focused still on his face, hands plucking at chicken wings. Pete knew she was waiting on stories, each day he had something different for her, something that happened right where they lived, some kind of wonder that confirmed miracles nothing at all but a regular occurrence of everyday life.

Pete took a sip from his beer, a forkful of pasta, checked

to make sure Lula was eating all right, having no problems other than dirty hands and face, food spattered all down her bib and some parts of her shirt.

Aspasia shook her head, almost bouncing in her seat, laughing.

"Come on, Pete. Stop playing. What happened today?"

"Hawk Eye almost got hit by a car."

Her eyes widened.

"I know you lying. Cars don't hit Hawk Eye. I mean, he just walk right in front of speeding cars all the time. He got some kind of immunity, I know he does."

"I'm telling you, he almost got hit by a car earlier."

"What happened then?"

Pete pushed his plate away, settled back in his chair, hugged his beer.

"Me and Red saw Hawk Eye walking on the shoulder of the highway this morning on the way to the site. Had to be what, about seven thirty in the morning and you know it was already smoking out there, and he was just walking like he had someplace to be and a certain time to be there. Me and Red waved and he gave us this kind of general's salute. Think of Private Benjamin, that's how silly he looked walking the shoulder like that, saluting people. Me and Red waved back, worried a minute about him being out there in all that sun and no trees, no nothing in sight to give some sort of shade, but Hawk Eye a grown man. Can't nobody make him do anything he don't want to do, and he really isn't hurting anybody, not even himself.

"We forgot all about him when we got to the site because working in hundred degree weather with humidity thrown on top makes it hard to just think straight. We forgot about him until lunchtime, when we saw him stumbling around the bend of the highway. And he was stumbling, too. I mean just falling all over his feet. It's what, a thirty-minute drive out to the site? He walked in all that heat, took him just about four hours so I guess he wasn't trying to win no race. So we all out there, me, Red, Vernon, a few other guys, eating our lunch under the shade of the building and here come Hawk Eye giving us all that same silly general salute, sitting down next to us and smiling, wiping sweat from his forehead. He was so sweaty all that wiping didn't make a bit of difference, didn't do nothing but spread more dirt over his face. I gave him some of my water and some of your cookies. Red gave him half his sandwich; Vernon gave him a piece of cold fried chicken. Hawk Eye inspected the building, took his time like he used to do some kind of construction work somewhere, ate real slow, wiped his hands on his shorts, studied the endless blue overhead.

"Then he said, 'I think this is my day, boys.'

"Red smacked him lightly on the head, like he been smacking most of us all our lives. 'Cut that boy shit out, man. This your day for what?'

"Red really likes Hawk Eye, used to date his mama when Hawk Eye was little and had a hand helping Hawk Eye grow up. Broke Red's heart that Hawk Eye wasn't never right again after the accident.

"Hawk Eye said, 'You know. Adios, see you later, final good-bye, going to lay down my sword and shield, all that.'

"Red was just puzzled, Vernon shook his head, some of the other guys rolled eyes and made faces.

"I said, 'What you talking about, Hawk? You talking about dying today?'

"Hawk Eye stretched his legs out in front of him, bent way over, straining and breathing hard the whole time, to touch his toes. 'Yup. That's what I'm talking about. That's what I'm talking about right there.'

"Vernon laughed at him. 'Hawk, you picked a piss poor day to die, I tell you that much.'

"Hawk Eye got up and threw his trash away, you know he's always polite. 'I didn't choose no day at all, the day choose me.'

"Red just watched him, trying to figure it out. 'What you going to do about it then? You tell me that.'

"Hawk Eye came back from the trash, stood over all of us, his shadow long and black behind him. 'Nothing I can do about it, Red. You know that. I know you know that.'

"Red sipped at his coke. 'Yeah, I guess I do.'

"Hawk Eye tapped the heels of his dirty tennis shoes together and saluted us. 'If I get over, I'll see you all tomorrow.'

"Vernon still just shook his head. 'Hope you get over then, brother.'

"Hawk Eye got back on the shoulder of the highway headed for town, and we all watched because he looked just as happy, not like he was thinking he was going to die any minute at all. We watching him and this lady in her Mercedes, I swear it had to be just off the lot, comes around the highway, veering to the shoulder. Some white lady with all this hair trying to put on makeup or something because she almost hits Hawk Eye. None of us moved, said a word, holding our breath because this was prophecy, you know? None of us was about to get in the way. Hawk Eye just stood there, never moved, didn't look like he even flinched. The Lady looked up at the last minute, slammed on her breaks and swerved around him, ended up a good few feet from the road.

"She jumped out her car, hollered to Hawk, 'You all right?'

Hawk Eye stared down at his feet like he was shocked he was still standing. 'I'm fine. Managed to get over, ain't that some shit?'

"The lady was on her knees, she was shaken so bad. Red went over to help her out. Hawk Eye saluted one last time and I guess he headed on in back to town."

Lula was slumped over in her high chair, nodding off, ready for bath and bed. Aspasia was wide eyed across the table from him, chewed slowly and thoughtfully at her lips.

"You mean that, what you said about Hawk Eye being a prophet?"

Pete cleared dirty dishes from the table, wiped down the old wood surface and cleaned Lula's high chair.

"I mean he got to be something, don't he?"

"People used to talk right after the accident. Something about him being able to predict when folks were going to pass. Then the more wild he became the more people certain he was just plain crazy, nothing special at all."

Pete picked up Lula's sleeping deadweight, her head resting like a rock against his shoulder.

"I don't know, Aspasia. That's just what happened today, that's all. I'm going to give Lula her bath and put her down. You got dishes?"

Aspasia rose slow from her chair, still chewing her lips, waving him away.

"Go ahead. I'll do dishes and clean up down here."

He carried Lula through the dim, hot house to the stairs. In the kitchen, Aspasia turned the CD player back on and Smokey Robinson sang "The Tears of a Clown." The middle of the '80s, nothing but rap and rhythm and blues on the radio and Aspasia never played anything current. Walking into the house was like walking into the '60s or the '70s. Most of the time Pete didn't mind, he had Run DMC and Dougie Fresh tapes strategically placed all inside the cab of his truck.

He ran lukewarm water for Lula, put her small body in

rising bubbles and foam. Lula stretched hands out over the bubbles, fingers spread wide, bubbles leaking out between spaces. She was quiet, which meant that she was more than ready for bed. There was nothing holding her up really, just his free hand around her small waist. His other hand moved the washcloth across her butter brown skin, brown with deep red undertones like candied yams just coming out the oven at Thanksgiving or Christmas. Lula half smiled at him as he lifted her to her feet to run wet cloth over her plump, dimpled bottom.

Pete wrapped her in a big, fluffy, white towel when he was done, laid her in the crib. He rubbed in lotion, massaging her small bones, getting at all the aches and pains she might have gotten during the day. Aspasia first turned him on to infant massage, made him take a class when Lula just barely new, screaming with colic, miserable at all times. Pete thought it was silly, grown men and women sitting around trying to find the right spots on infants, not enough arm and leg or chest or back to even rub good, babies the absolute center of everyone's existence. He took the class before he realized he'd been duped badly, when he was still thinking that all he had to do was put in eighteen good years and let go. The class was the first hint that putting in good years a little more than he expected and letting go impossible.

Lula was sleep hard before he got her diaper on. He put her in a light sleeper and made sure ice wind coming from the air conditioner was not too cold. She had a night lamp, some cute, girly thing Mama picked up in Cleveland with dancing fairies and moon and stars. He turned it on and stars and moon skipped in circles across the shadowed ceiling. Lula slept like an angel child, brown cheeks rounded and smooth, eyelashes long and curving and black against brown skin. The responsibility of it all often overwhelmed

Eden, Ohio

him, his palms damp and his mouth dry thinking about
keeping her safe and healthy and all right from now until.
He knew girl children were easy to damage and easy to hurt
and easy to leave unraveling at the seams for the rest of their
lives.

Aspasia was in bed two-strand twisting her hair. Hair
thick and black and all over her head, didn't hang straight
at all unless she put it in braids or twists. Her clothes were
gone and she was sitting on the bed in his boxers and T-
shirt. The room was already cool from the air conditioner
in the window. It was just after eight thirty and outside the
sun beginning to go down, bright blue sky dulled to gray.
Pete sprawled out on the bed, watching her.

"You want me to help with your hair?"

"No, thanks. I remember the last time you helped. My
hair a hot mess and tangled for days."

The stereo playing jazz, Coltrane's "Niama," song from
one of the albums Daddy gave him before he went back to
New York. Pete loved albums the same way Daddy loved albums, cleaned them once a week, sat down lazy Sundays to
read the inside of album covers, stare, fascinated, at album
artwork. The bedroom done in soft greens, multi-colored
throw rug thrown across the floor at the foot of their bed.
The quilt from the bed folded and placed in the cherry wood
chest, handed down from mama to child and mama to child
for forever, in the corner. Nothing but cool cotton white
sheet thrown over the bed, fat pillows scattered against the
headboard. Pete put his head in her lap, looked up at her
brown skin, the curve of her throat and neck. Her hands
stopped twisting, rested lightly along his scalp.

"No, keep doing your hair. I just want to lie with you a
minute like this."

"It's okay. My hair can wait."

The sun almost gone in the sky and outside children and people came alive again, laughed all up and down the street, radios pulled out onto porches and music like the scent of summer flowers in the air. Pete's head heavy in Aspasia's lap, her fingers moved slow across his scalp, rubbed lightly along his temple, the bridge of his nose, his mouth. His eyes closed and he felt the warm white gold of her engagement ring against his skin.

"When you think we need to start planning our wedding?"

Her hands moved down his neck to massage his shoulders and upper chest.

"No rush. I'm not going anywhere. You?"

He kissed the palms of both her hands. "No, but I want to get married."

"We need to save a little bit more. Your mama said she'd help us out, but I don't want to lean on her like that."

"What you think? By early fall?"

"All right. Let's start thinking about dates and all that stuff. I swear I don't want no big, out-of-hand thing."

"What's the point if you don't have something like that?"

Aspasia pushed his head from her lap, laid down next to him, the full length of their bodies touching.

"You're a man. You can say that. Remember when Sharon was planning her wedding? Vernon was no help. By the time the wedding came she was just about bald and had to wear extensions. You remember?"

Pete rolled his thigh over her legs; she scooted deeper into the mattress.

"That's Sharon's craziness. She lost her mind, had to have matching this and nothing quite right, stressed herself out. Besides, you got too much hair to go bald anyway."

"You think Jeremiah will be here until the wedding?"

"I hope so. You know he'll be the best man."

"Yes. I know."

The record was at the end, needle scratching like hum of insects kept outdoors because all the windows closed. The air conditioner let out a steady, familiar whine. Pete pulled reluctantly away, turned the radio and lights off, went back to bed, curled into Aspasia back to front, the sweet smelling thickness of her hair soft in his face.

"You and Lula had a good day?"

Aspasia hands rested lightly against his forearm.

"Me and Lula are fine. Thank God we over that infant stage. All that crying and no smiles from her, no laughter, no anything to let us know that we're doing okay and not ruining her for life. I couldn't stand it."

"Me neither. Nothing cute about a screaming-all-the-time child."

Aspasia laughed.

"Hush. My baby was too cute."

Later on, the air conditioner still whined, Aspasia snored lightly, Lula slept hard down the hall, and Pete woke up with salty wet cheeks. His heartbeat slow, his breath shallow, some unknown thing in his dreams, floating on icy wind from the air conditioner.

Chapter Fourteen

Friday mornings were like any other week day morning for old people just retired and used to getting up when stars still in the sky like blinking lightning bugs to rush to some job that just paid enough. No way for Vern to stop her eyes from opening like invisible strings were attached at five every morning. Red Cap long since gone to go fishing on Lake Erie. Red Cap all the time in search of peace and quiet after a week filled with loud noise and the general chaos at construction sites. Red took off Fridays, rolled out of bed, feet whispered across the floor, and water fell from the shower silent. He cooked breakfast with lights dimmed and no hint of grease popping. He never made a sound.

Vern pulled and pushed at covers, buried her head under pillows, counted the small deep cracks in the orange of her ceiling, watched her ceiling fan rotate slowly above her head. No sleep, just a body used to doing the same thing day in and day out for thirty-something years. The habit was permanent and bred deep into her skin the same way she had her mama's eyes and her daddy's long fingers.

Jeremiah was on his way home, sleep somewhere along

the highway on the Greyhound bus, each mile huge black wheels traveled stealing another pound from his flesh because no way to turn back time, no way to avoid the unavoidable. He didn't call her, for him not to call meant nothing for her to do but hold his hand like she used to when he was a little boy and constantly tried to run away, laughing and giggling, in crowded parking lots. Jeremiah with his bright smile, and lazy eyes, and joy, so filled with joy that miles along the highway stealing pounds and pounds from his flesh nothing less than tragic. When he left Eden for Brooklyn for good all those years ago Vern's breast had leaked tiny amounts of mother's milk. Mother's milk wet the front of her shirt for an entire day, made her embarrassed to leave the house at all. She had cradled her breasts and thought all that day about the lost of her baby child.

Vern pulled herself out of bed, body stiff from sleeping on covers damp with sweat and the ceiling fan blowing insistently against her. Just stiffness, no arthritis like most of her friends, no pains that wouldn't go away or required medication. Her body couldn't do the same things anymore, no running from here to there with a baby on the hip and bags from the market in hand. She didn't look the same, parts of her loose and hanging like she was someone's old rag doll.

Vern stood in front of the mirror on her closet door, naked, skin shiny and loose with age, and missed the woman she was thirty years ago. She thought back to thirty years ago and her boys still babies and her first husband still around and loving hard every part and piece of her black skin. Her first husband talked to her, against her night after night when the boys in their own rooms sleep. Just the two of them buried beneath covers like covers stacked and piled high kept everything out and all the goodness of skin rubbing against skin private, something just for them. He whispered against her thigh, against the underside of her breasts, his voice like the blues and jazz records he loved, smooth, persuasive, and insistent.

"Baby. You my pretty black baby. What I need with anything else when I got a woman at home with skin like licorice or chocolate icing spread across some cake."

She didn't have the sense to know then that good sex not the same as commitment, that good sex turned dull when bills weren't paid and the house went unclean for days because instead of a husband she had another child, another little boy. Little boy who pulled at her skirts, her hair, dug in her pockets for loose change, sat belligerently at the breakfast table waiting on food. Her head ached all the time, all the time a tightness in her chest, one long continuous panic attack. The only time her lungs gathered air was in bed when he touched her. His fingers strong and sure, his mouth soft and moist, and he took his time, used to listening to records over and over, reading music or practicing a song until he got it just right. First time he touched her, music inside him raced out, filled her with melody and beat and she knew what he wanted from her, knew he wanted her to sing, an extension of his horn.

She was charmed to be more than quick release, shallow pleasure, let his music inside her until nothing left but the force of his breath constantly blowing at her, constantly making her flesh subtle and weak, wanting. Three babies in four years the result of wanting, wanting like her body and mind nothing more than musical notes flying random in the air, waiting to be grabbed, placed in some kind of order, forced to make sense.

Three babies in four years meant mouths always at her

breasts, milk always flowing, belly always round and hard. She didn't like the leak and mess of milk, pearl white stained her underwear and clothes, embarrassed her in public when she felt large wet circles forming around nipples. Three babies in four years and she was overwhelmed, didn't have time to think, dreamed of just getting up and leaving while babies sucked peaceful and warm at her breasts. Worried about making more babies when he came to her at night, hands firm, mouth persuasive. The force of his breath shaped her into a well-loved, well-remembered tune.

She never knew music supposed to make her feel good could make her feel so heavy, weighted down by babies and the firm smooth weight of his hands against her stretch-marked flesh. She grew tired of being his "Sunday Kind of Love" and "Trouble in Mind" and "Don't Let the Sun Catch You Crying." Her body a dumping ground for sad jazz and sadder blues and Vern knew he found beauty in all the sad, but beauty wasn't enough. She wanted some joy, she wanted some bills paid and some dishes done and some clothes washed and a husband who didn't shudder or laugh at the very idea of being a grown-up.

She still remembered conversations, fights over breakfast once the boys went to school or out to play, in bed after lovemaking, her head still humming whatever tune he wanted her to be for the night.

"I need more help."

Help because she was drowning and three sets of little boy hands holding tight to her hair, around her throat, his hand trying to shove her head completely under.

"You know I do what I can."

His "do what I can" meant sometimes going to work and sometimes staying home, pretending he didn't hear children cry, locking himself in the bedroom or the basement to listen to records or practice with his horn.

"I can't do this."

"You love me?"

His hands on her and the music started.

"I love you."

"You love my babies?"

The music loud and insistent and no way for her to make it stop, she tried closing her eyes, concentrated on bright lights dancing behind closed lids.

"I love my children. Yes."

"Then what's the problem?"

Her head ached and he followed winding tears along her cheeks, the corners of her mouth, waterfalls over the bump of her chin.

"That's not the point."

It certainly wasn't the point when she kicked him out the house, watched his face collapse and his hands reach for her even as she moved away. She gave him privacy to say good-bye to the boys, didn't lay any blame at his feet, helped him iron and pack clothes, drove him to the Greyhound bus station, waved good-bye to him with tears clouding her vision and relief crowding her heart.

Vern got out of bed and went to the shower, warm water dug into her skin, over the short curls of her graying Afro. The smell of Red Cap's shaving lotion still in the bathroom, lemon and musk, the scent pleasant as she soaped and scrubbed, thought about her children and grandchild and how no good luck stayed with her family from generation to generation, nothing to do but straighten the back, lift the load. People in her family, especially the men, quick to die and died fantastic, horrible deaths. Murders and suicides, vicious love triangles, obscene carelessness, subtle or incurable diseases. Eden cemetery filled with her people north to south and east to west, bodies of her people made grass green and soil lush. Her people were, to an alarming degree, the soil of Eden, the salt of the earth. Her oldest boy, Quincy, buried there, his body nothing more than fodder, his memory faded, tarnished, the only bright glow his childhood.

First babies were different from the last. Vern had Quincy when she was twenty and just married. Brought him home and there was absolute terror, the numbing worry that she was always on the verge of hurting her child. She closed her eyes when she picked him up because if Quincy fell from her arms, fell from her clumsy and not motherlike fingers she surely didn't want to see it. She didn't bathe him for a month. Thoughts of Quincy's little brown face lost under slightly warm water and suds left her hands dead on the bathtub faucets. When feeding him she listened for the slight grunts and sucking noises that babies supposed to make, watching his face to see if it changed colors, imagining milk going down the wrong way and how would she know because she had no idea what a choking baby looked or sounded like.

Despite the worry and the anxiety there was sweetness, to look into his round face and see her eyes and her husband's mouth and Mama's nose. She held him night after night after night against her chest, made sure their bellies moved in tandem. His baby-warm breath left chill bumps along her flesh, baby-soft hair like kitten fur rubbed against her. One baby not the same as three or even two and she was never rushed, never felt like Quincy needed more than humanely possible to give, despite his tantrums and demanding cries.

Her boys, especially Quincy, were close to grown when

their daddy left. She didn't consider problems, didn't have any idea that raising a boy into some kind of man all by herself was the same as crossing fingers and hoping for the best, carrying rabbit's feet and four-leaf clovers in pockets and wishing on unbearably bright shooting stars.

Vern left the shower, rubbed her body with a thick blue towel that she had washed earlier in the week and left outside to dry. The miserable sun in the sky and heat constantly smacking at exposed faces, legs, arms, knees at least good for drying clothes on the line running through the backyard. She moisturized her body with lavender infused oil, put oil between her hands and let hands wander through the soft thickness of her short Afro. She loved hair when she was younger, wore hair permed straight down the back, pulled into loose buns at the nape of her neck, simple and braided away from her face. Now she liked her hair short, liked no fuss, and hair that looked undeniable perfect when she got up in the morning, when she went to bed at night, when she swam in the lake or in the pool at the community center. She went back to the bedroom, searched the closet, dressed in a cool, flowing skirt and sleeveless shirt.

Red Cap left bacon and biscuits warming in the oven. Red Cap didn't mind cooking, didn't mind cleaning, didn't mind doing any small thing that might make her life a little easy, make her get up in the morning with smiles flirting at the corners and edges of her mouth.

She ate slowly, bacon slightly cool and congealed grease formed around the plate, biscuits still soft. She spread strawberry jams on her biscuits, watched morning shadows hop across dark tiled floors as she ate.

Jeremiah was coming home, every second he was closer, every second farther and farther away, out of reach and still always her giggling baby. Pete was born serious and kind,

Quincy reckless and a little mean, but Jeremiah was nothing but sweet. Amazed her how children were the exact same people from cradle to grave, just got better at being whatever they were. There was no way at all for her to even fake surprise when Quincy moved down to Cleveland and started selling drugs. She never had enough for Quincy, he always wanted more. It started at the breast, her milk left him voracious and demanding and she had to supplement breast milk with formula. Quincy moved when he was eighteen because he was tired of her rules, tired of her nagging, tired of getting up to face the same old tired town, same old tired people.

And there was no way at all for her to fake surprise when Quincy was brought home in a body bag, face completely blown off, no way to identify her child except dental records and fingerprints. She knew the men in her family died young, knew old women in Eden whispered about retribution for sins committed generations and generations ago by her kin. Sins that no one in Eden could quite remember, except Eliza who seemed to remember or know everything. Sins that were so hideous they made the act of remembering obscene. Sins passed from generation to generation like the name "Jeremiah," which had been in the family since before time.

Jeremiah on his way home, body still warm to the touch and sweet smile still spreading slow across his face but it didn't matter because the end result was no different, just a little more time.

Quincy was special because he was the first and Jeremiah was special because Vern had known that he was the last pregnancy, that there were no more babies sitting patient and still in her womb waiting to come out. Vern was in her mid-twenties and her marriage beat at her chest, confused and displaced all internal organs, and she still had two babies in diapers.

The walls of the kitchen painted cloud blue and the tiled floor beneath Vern's feet dull with time and age, the house passed from generation to generation in Red's family the same as the house that she inherited from Mama that now belonged to Pete. She used to come to this house with Mama when she was a girl to visit; she remembered how the floors looked when she was a girl, shining and supple, slick with care.

Last babies gave off some kind of smell, different from all the before babies. Smell that she breathed in deep and felt her whole body relax, like smell the same as strong, pampered hands giving a slow massage at an expensive salon. She didn't mind last babies who were fussy, grumpy, cried all the time, didn't sleep through the night, impossible to leave even for a minute with someone else. Nothing but patience because last babies only babies for a year or two at most and then anxious to be grown, pulling their hands away in parking lots and shopping malls, refusing to be held or rocked to sleep, looking around at the world like all they needed was themselves, no mama at all.

Vern knew when she held her last baby all night long, rocked Jeremiah from morning to night, kept him at the breast continuously those first few weeks when her nipples cracked and bleeding and about to fall off that she was rocking a part of herself away.

She spent hours, days, weeks sitting in bed or on the couch rocking and rocking and singing and singing and hushing and hushing and not minding because she was rocking and singing and hushing that part of herself slipping away with each pound her last baby gained, with each new thing that Jeremiah learned and did over and over and over until he learned something else.

The possibility of mama was being sucked out with all the time and attention and care for a little person recently separate from her. It was hard to tell, when she held her Jeremiah, where his soft, lush, baby skin begin and her rough, dry, skin-smelling-like-drugstore-merry-berries-lotion began.

Chapter Fifteen

Brutal summer heat coupled with the statewide drought was nothing less than hell on Eliza's garden. Flowers wilted and faded, color washed out by sun's lemon yellow intensity. Herbs withered and dried in the ground. Dark, rich earth begged for water and the only time watering gardens allowed in the entire state was early Saturday mornings from 6:00 A.M. to 10:00 A.M. She understood the cycles of nature, knew that death made way for life and life made way for death continuously since well before time. Knew the slow death of her garden from dehydration as natural as ninety-degree days in mid December because cycles of life and death, of nature, in no way at all predictable.

She tried when she was young and just coming into her powers as a woman to tell futures and hold off the inevitable. She failed completely—the harder she tried to control the world around her the more confusing the world became. She grew exhausted trying to keep husbands at home, away from houses of girlfriends and mistresses, exhausted trying to keep children safe from any and all accidents (cars, buses, long falls from flights of stairs), exhausted trying to keep people she loved from finding pain waiting unexpectedly in empty cereal bowls at the breakfast table, in bathtubs filled with scented bubbles. She remembered what Mama told her before she died, when she wondered why Mama just didn't will herself better with the power of the blood, power of all the before Eliza's rampant in her flesh.

Mama smiled at her from her bed, laughed a little at her arrogance.

"What we are, what we've got can't change the inevitable, baby. Some things are just going to be no matter what we do or don't do. The things we can change are small when you think about it, when you think about God giving life to everything we see. The big things, the inevitable things are completely out of our hands. Me sick in this bed is just inevitable."

She remembered those words when Daddy died when she was seventeen and she was left with no one but Aspasia and Aspasia still a child, still looking to her to fill every need and most wants. Inevitable the same as doing what needed to be done, facing what needed to be faced. She thought of those words now in the quiet of her house, thought about Jeremiah on his way home, his homecoming as inevitable as stars viciously burning themselves out in black skies.

Jeremiah was always underfoot as a little boy, he and Aspasia best friends despite the difference of sex. Their friendship managed to hold through childhood and puberty, didn't unravel when Jeremiah moved to New York and rarely came home. Jeremiah, as a child, was so sweet that she sometimes wanted to serve him with milk. His smile was always easy on his face, lighting his eyes. He wasn't one of those little boys always busy pulling girls' hair, tying empty soda cans to the tails of defenseless cats, getting into all kinds of trouble because nothing else in Eden for boys to do. He moved slow in the world. Somehow realized that every step he took, every decision he made, capable of hurting or helping someone else, a sensitive child.

Aspasia, Jeremiah, and Hawk Eye liked to play in the yard, climbed trees, build forts using pillows from the living room sofa, had sword fights with long and brittle twigs. She used to cook dinner at the stove and watch them from the kitchen window, enjoying their childhood because her childhood was as good as over when she turned thirteen, when Mama died. They ran wild, laughing and carefree, and she envied their lack of worries, no bills, no meals to fix, no clothes to buy, no child to keep healthy and whole. They played like their entire lives devoted to seeing how fast legs and feet could move, how often brown bodies could flip and tumble over green grass. They were comfortable and happy in their skins because they knew she was watching over them.

Eliza sat at the kitchen table and thoughts of Jeremiah formed tightness in her throat, made cool herbal tea hard to get down. She knew all about Jeremiah the same way she knew all about everyone in Eden. She knew his bloodlines as well as she knew her own, knew that his blood carried the possibility of redemption just as her blood carried the ability to heal. He was the direct descendant of Jeremiah Baker who bloodied his hands first on that long ago night when the sun came early to Eden. In her head she gathered recipes and prayers, magic empowered with divinity, the only real magic anywhere in the world. She wondered over what she could and couldn't do to help him face the inevitable.

The kitchen was bright even though early morning sun was just rising in clear expanse of blue, all the lights turned off to help with the heat. The kitchen cooler now than it would be at midday when she would sit down to eat vegetable salad for lunch with sweat gathered between her breasts, weeping from the back of her legs, her hairline. She usually went to dinner at Aspasia's or any one of the older women in Eden, widowed and wanting company.

She ate alone, tried not to let the quiet of the house overwhelm her, concentrated on other noises. The sound of light heat wind, raspy and annoying came in through the window and back-door screens, she imagined the sound like heat wind billowing sand across long stretches of desert. The house was old, built long before the first World War, all the pipes old, must be replaced soon. From the corner of the kitchen came steady drip of water from old faucet, constant and soothing, staining the kitchen sink.

She ate slow but efficiently. She had an errand to run, someone she needed to pick up and she didn't want to be late.

She hummed to herself, Mahalia Jackson's "How I Got Over" and every now and then she smiled, picturing Mahalia performing and shouting and all ladylike giving praises to the Lord. She thought of her childhood, the general feel of it all, the peace and wholeness of life then. That was before everything, before growing up. She wanted to be a child again, just for a moment to feel the security and love. Children never really appreciated their days, they just kind of raced through like the joy was guaranteed and the days endless.

The house reminded her of Mama. All the old furniture Mama picked out after her great-grandfather died. In the living room there was the huge sofa. It was used well over the years and had the permanent imprints of people's behinds to prove it. Eliza loved the sofa. It wasn't even furniture, but an old friend, a place to rest when moving on seemed impossible, not to mention pointless. The couch had seen her family through the good times and the bad. When Mama was sick, Daddy used to bring her downstairs in the living room and lay her on those soft, giving cushions so that she could watch television or talk to the many guests—because everyone loved Mama—that visited.

The house was quiet.

There was a time when you couldn't buy quiet in the house. The house, when she was a little girl, was filled with life, her mama and daddy teasing one another or fighting, she and Aspasia tumbling and playing upon hardwood floors. There were sleepovers and birthday parties and Daddy, although the majority of his attention was centered on Mama, sometimes took her for long walks and spun her in the air until she was dizzy and laughing.

In early spring and continuing throughout the summer, Eliza worked in her garden each Saturday. The earth of the garden was moist, soft, sensually warm. Like a naked body, and Eliza let her hands wander aimlessly through it, shifting, constantly shifting. The black earth moving beneath her fingers mesmerized her.

People walking by were struck by her beauty, because in her garden, among all those sweet-smelling flowers, Eliza was herself—completely natural and stunning. Her clothes and hands and face were smudged with dirt, and sweat was running all down her making her skin glow. Her skin beneath the sunlight resembled a ripe peach, all bright yellows with just a hint of red and pink. The warm earth made it all seem simple.

She remembered things in the garden, while listening to the hum of insects and her own voice whispering a song. There was the time Aspasia made her lunch for school. She was only about nine, so Aspasia had to be about seven or so. The lunch was horrible, a lunch that only a child would think to make. There was a jelly sandwich with the jelly just running over the sides, a chocolate cake squashed into a plastic bag, and a candy bar. Eliza hated jelly and wasn't a huge fan of chocolate cake, but because her sister made it she ate every bit of it.

It was good.

There was the time Aspasia had a horrible cold, just sneezing and sniffling and all around miserable. Mama and Daddy weren't concerned really. They gave her medicine and chicken soup, but that was it. Eliza was sick with worry. She stayed home from school, hovering over Aspasia's bedside, making sure that she was comfortable and breathing. She was certain that Aspasia was near death.

At night during the winter the wind was a harsh, frightening thing. Eliza hated the thought of her sister sleeping in her room alone, sick and sad and listening to the wind. Eliza stripped off Aspasia's clothes and then her own—the cool night air touching her child's body. She climbed into bed with Aspasia, drew Aspasia's body close to her naked flesh. She felt the heat and intimacy, wallowed in it with absolute abandon. Her hands traveled across the skin of Aspasia's back and shoulders, traced the contours and lines of her face, entangled in the soft, oiled thickness of her hair. Aspasia clung to her, arms tight around her, breath smelling of chicken noodles and cough syrup beating against her neck.

She asked, lips moving against Aspasia's ear. "Are you okay? You warm enough?"

Aspasia responded as if she were drugged. "I can't breathe, my chest hurts."

She was immediately concerned. "Did Mama put the Vics rub on it?"

"Can't you smell it? But it still hurts . . ."

Eliza pulled her closer. "Just hush. Don't think about it. Mommy says that if you don't think about it, it'll go away."

"All right. And . . ." Aspasia coughed, shuddering throughout her entire body.

"Do you want me to get Mamma? Aspasia? You want me to go get Mamma?" She questioned, alarmed.

"No, you stay with me . . ." Aspasia started to cry.

"Okay." She held her tighter.

"Stay with me . . ."

"Okay . . . Okay. You warm enough?"

"Don't leave."

They dug in the mud after thunderstorms, the mud warm and soft; they buried themselves in it. They played house and Mama went to work and built and tore down bridges in the yard. They had tea parties and picnics and went cruising the neighborhood on their bikes. They went to the creek behind the high school to try and catch crayfish, lost themselves in the green surrounding the town, tripping over branches and grass so high almost to their waists.

Eliza pushed her chair back from the kitchen table, left her dirty dishes in the sink and walked through the house to the front door. There were answers to the future tied to her memories of childhood, tied to Aspasia, Hawk Eye, and Jeremiah. Particularly Jeremiah. It was almost like there was a veil over her face, a light flimsy thing that nevertheless prevented her from actually seeing. She grabbed her car keys and headed out into the early morning. When Jeremiah left Eden that first time there was a small earthquake, cups shook in cabinets and plates danced slightly across tables. Eliza knew then that he would be back, and wondered what offering he would bring when he finally returned to Eden for eternity. Every child of Eden eventually stayed, no mat-

ter if they wanted to or not. Eliza had spent many slow afternoons and evenings at the gravesites of family and
friends, listening to whispers from the forgotten mass grave
buried deep in Eden's subconscious, staring down at soft
green grass and solid cement markers, wondering how
much innocent blood was needed.

Chapter Sixteen

It was dark outside tinted Greyhound bus windows, never-ending rain fell like uncontrollable tears from dark skies. Large raindrops pounded against the hood and sides of the bus. Jeremiah tried to get comfortable, forced his body to relax into hard and awkward contours of the bus seat. His neck tightened from the strain of overnight bus ride, most of his muscles stiff and useless. He swayed unsteady on his feet, from side to side each time he went to the back of the bus to use the rest room.

The majority of other passengers were fast asleep, snores loud and persistent over the hum from the bus's air conditioners. Some passengers had feet resting easy in the aisle, heads propped up by backpacks and handbags against the windows. The only other person not asleep was the teenage girl in front of him with bloodred nails. She still had her earphones on, head still swayed lazily with music he could no longer hear because she had turned the volume down. She popped her gum softly in the darkness, drummed her fingers lightly against tinted windows. He envied her, her whole life ahead, no reason to look back.

He settled back in the seat, closed his eyes. Always there dancing, sensual, smiling New York women burned bright against the dull red of his lids. They smiled at him and invited him to dance, held out arms to him, pouted lips, rolled shoulders and hips. Jeremiah knew there were no more dances for him, for the rest of his life he would be the man standing in the corner alone, the solitary wallflower.

The history of his family was one of endless lapses in judgment and early deaths. He worried about death as a child, made up rhymes to keep death away, pleaded with God at night on bended knees for death to somehow quietly pass him by. He had thought that it was Eden, the rich soil, and the deep green. He knew that there was something in the earth that marked Eden as fallen because he had found it as a child with Hawk Eye and Aspasia. He had left for Brooklyn to avoid his own mortality, and in Brooklyn it caught up with him and grabbed him by the throat.

When he first got the news from men and women in white coats with his imminent death smeared like white milk moustaches all across their faces that he tested positive, he was stunned. He got tested because almost every sexually active adult in New York was worried over a virus with no cure, a virus that rotted bodies from the inside out, left strong, healthy people suddenly weak and defenseless, target for any minor or major illness floating in the air like pollution from large factories and greedy, gas-guzzling cars. He never expected to test positive. He was careful with his sexual partners, not all the time. He figured out too late that not all the time was enough for white coats to talk to him in slow, soothing voices, stare at him with pity and the confirmation of his death leaking from their eyes.

He left pristine, doctor's offices dazed. Walked around Manhattan, through Central Park, tried to imagine vicious alien virus raging rampant in the interior of his flesh, stubbornly searching out and destroying all his body's natural defenses. He sat on well-tended green grass of Central Park far away from other people, his body a time bomb, in no way fit to be near healthy, whole persons. He was on his lunch break from the graphic design office, and he never went back. He sat in the park, watched the sun stroll across the sky, counted his breaths, cried.

He was depressed for weeks, suicidal depression and just to be sure he threw away razors in the bathroom, got rid of sleeping pills, hid kitchen knives in locked cabinets. He took vacation time from work, drank vodka and gin straight from the bottle for lunch, woke up in the mornings thirsty for merlot like red wine the same as orange juice, the perfect way to start the day.

He woke up one morning, looked in the mirror, realized he was the same exact person as before. Nothing was wrong with him but a hangover and sloppy beard and mustache that needed to be shaved down. Men and women in white coats were wrong when they looked at him with pity and death leaking from their eyes. He was no closer to death now than he had been before positive test came back. He showered, shaved with his electric razor, dressed, and went to work. He walked the streets en route to the subway, watched other people. They didn't know a thing, couldn't tell that he was diagnosed as rotten inside. They smiled at him, stepped politely out his way, or cut rudely in front of him. They snarled fed-up frowns, went oblivious about their New York City business.

He understood then that he was like the proverbial tree in the forest, if no one knew he was ill, if no one was there when tests results were revealed, was he really sick? Was there really anything wrong with him?

He arrived at his office whistling, pleasant smile on his face. He went about his regular New York City business like every other New Yorker and as days passed and no one stopped him on the street, ran him off subway platforms or out of taxi cabs, restaurants, and clubs, it became easier and easier to pretend.

Three months after positive test he was lounging in night clubs, taking dates out to brunch and dinner, no symptoms, no illness, not even common colds and runny noses. He was living the life he was meant to live; young, black, successful, urban professional, living the life for which he had left Eden and moved to New York. He met Nia in a swanky New York City club at the very beginning of summer when New York air still somewhat fresh from the rains of spring. Music roared from huge speakers at either end of the room, beat demanding and rhythmic. Hip hop was just beginning its short race to becoming America's music. He nodded his head to the beat, sipped his beer at the bar, attempted to scream a conversation with a few of his coworkers. Nia stood in a corner by herself, expensive clothes, hair, jewelry as if she had no one else to spend her money on, no one else to give surprises and extravagant gifts.

He excused himself from his coworkers, walked across the room for her, watched her straighten her back and lift her chin, preparing for another round. The defensiveness of her stance made him sad, swamped by great wave of tenderness. He wanted to be kind to her because it appeared as if not many men were.

"Hello. How are you?"

The simplicity of the greeting threw her, he could see it in her face. She was expecting word games, male posturing.

"Fine. Thank you."

He leaned into her, smelled her expensive perfume, rose petals and musk, hints of citrus.

"Can I buy you a drink?"

She considered him through long dark lashes, her face well and tastefully done like models at runway shows.

"Yes, please. Thank you."

She was slim and sturdy, rounded and soft, deep dark skin, high cheekbones and wide mouth, beautiful.

"What are you drinking?"

She shrugged her shoulders, her fighter's posture relaxed slightly. He knew she hoped he wasn't gay, married, just out of prison, otherwise engaged.

"Just merlot."

"Okay, merlot it is then."

They were inseparable the entire short summer. She was a school teacher at a public school, taught pre-kindergarten and kindergarten, spent her days in classrooms full of four- and five-year-old children and loved every moment. He asked her about her job the first time they went to dinner at a well–air-conditioned Ethiopian restaurant to avoid brutal summer heat.

She tore apart fluffy, semi-bitter Ethiopian bread, used bread to scoop up spicy dishes of shrimp and lentils.

"I play all day, basically. Get to draw and finger paint and build blocks and match pictures and dress doll babies and play house. We read books and try to introduce kids to really basic skills—how to hold a pen, count to a hundred, say and recognize all the letters of the alphabet and the letters in their names. But the really, really great thing about teaching children so young is that everything can be made into some kind of game, some kind of fun thing to hold their interest and keep them involved. I love it."

He sipped at fresh-squeezed mango juice, sweetness and

coldness sliding down his throat, watched while she talked. She was from a small suburb outside of Philadelphia, not a native New Yorker. She reminded him of Mama and all the old women who helped raise him in Eden. She was that easy and comfortable in her skin, ease that made kindness and graciousness natural for her, politeness bred deep in skin and bones. He loved the way she talked, well-bred, well-raised accent specific to Philadelphia suburbs. He listened to her for hours, stories about her children, the five or so years she'd been in New York, how much she grew to love the city once she realized that it wasn't a huge metropolis at all but a whole bunch of small distinct neighborhoods and towns, people living and trying to enjoy and maybe understand their lives like anywhere else.

He liked her stories about her boy students best, boys always in trouble, pulling girls' hair, wandering, easily distracted at museums and city zoos, roughhousing in the middle of the classroom like they were at the playground, racing through their small blocks or small backyards at home.

Nia taught pre-kindergarten class that entire summer. She went to school in comfortable skirts or shorts, safe, flat shoes that covered her toes, easy-to-clean blouses and T-shirts. She came home smelling like milk, cookies, fresh fruit, crayons, finger paints, brightly colored Play-doh. Sometimes he caught her before she changed into her after-school clothes, before she showered with sweet smelling soap, sprayed on expensive rose, musk, citrus perfume. He liked her just home from school, loosely held her in his arms, all the good days of childhood rising like cakes or fresh-baked bread from memory, forming great lumps in his throat, need for simplicity in his heart. He realized while holding her, her face against his cheek, her hands stained with paint and markers around his waist, that he loved her. Love deep and wide like love between parent and child, love between brother and sister, didn't realize it was possible to love a woman until he stood with her resting light and happy in his embrace.

He never took her to bed, although he wanted to, thought about touching her at night after he delivered her to the front door of her apartment with tenderness and kisses. He pretended nothing was different, everything the same as before positive test, but deep inside he knew. He was afraid to give to anyone else what had carelessly been given to him. She didn't seem to mind, relieved not to fight off viselike arms, wandering, persistent hands. He knew she was thinking of him as more than quick pleasure never heard from again. He kissed her lips, the arch of her eyebrows, the long length of her neck, the soft child's space between her collarbones. Wrapped arms around her sturdy body, wondered over the shine and smoothness of her skin, the most beautiful woman he had ever known in life, certainly only woman he had ever really loved and he couldn't have her.

They wandered New York all that summer, went to movies and plays and restaurants and museums and art galleries, anyplace well-air conditioned to avoid stifling heat. New York became more and more miserable further and further into summer. Everyone tired from the heat, standing in long lines for shaved ice, adults and children running mad through spraying fire hydrants. Air-conditioned laundromats became neighborhood hangout spots, people without air conditioning in small apartments slept out on fire escapes for night breezes, anything to cool off. Skyscrapers beneath the bright glare of sun shiny like towers and towers of glass.

Jeremiah went to meet Nia at her apartment to go for ice

cream at the end of the summer, late August and New York stubbornly holding tight to summer, refusing to slide gracefully into fall.

She lived in Brooklyn and he waited patiently at the stoop of her brownstone apartment building.

She came out the apartment smiling, kissed him lightly on the mouth. She tasted like toothpaste, mouthwash.

"Hello, Jeremiah. And how was your day?"

She used her teacher's voice to amuse him and he laughed.

"Just fine. And yours?"

She sighed, rolled her eyes.

"We lost a child today at the zoo. We found him eventually, but it was a complete mess for a while there."

"How unteacher like of you."

She swatted at him playfully, smile widened across her face.

"Don't make jokes; don't laugh, it's really not that funny."

Nia was already changed from her standard casual school uniform, already showered, smell of crayons and milk and Play-doh replaced with clean-scented soap, expensive citrus, musk rose perfume. Her hair pulled back in a ponytail off the neck, pretty floral summer dress giggled and danced over her roundness.

"You're right. What happened?"

"It was one of the boys . . ."

"Isn't it always?"

"Yeah, well, it was one of the boys and he just wandered off. We had them holding hands in pairs of two, neatly lined up, behaving okay, nothing too wild. Looked around and Keith, the little boy, was just gone. Took us an hour to find him, had to go to security and everything. You know I was terrified. I don't know even know how to begin to tell a parent that I lost their child."

"Where was he?"

"Guess."

"Roaring at lions, hissing at reptiles?"

"Nope. He was making faces at the monkeys."

"That would have been my next guess."

"Yeah, right."

"No, it really would have been my next guess."

They walked to the neighborhood ice-cream parlor, his hand lightly cradling her elbow, their hips rubbing against each other. They smiled at New Yorkers stumbling about with ice-cold juices and sodas in their hands. Women with hair pulled back from the face, short shorts and thin-strapped sandals and T-shirts that showed large slices of midriffs, hints of breasts. Men with heads shaved bald or baseball caps bent at the rim and white muscle shirts. Everyone looked wilted, drained by the heat, faces flushed and healthy sheen of sweat lighting glow just underneath skin.

The neighborhood ice-cream parlor was full, families with small children trying to keep children from creating huge ice-cream messes. They sat outside at one of the small tables for two the parlor provided, pretty small table with a single fake rose sitting tired in a cheap, plastic vase.

Ice cream cool against his mouth, his teeth ached and his lips pleasantly numb. He licked at a plain butter pecan cone and Nia worked her way through a chocolate sugar cone. They watched a harassed mother and half asleep father try to calm a screaming toddler hysterical because all the ice cream gone.

Nia smiled like a screaming baby perfectly acceptable, in no way hurt eardrums or ruined the night.

"You want kids, Jeremiah?"

He froze, and butter pecan ice cream melted fast, dripped down the backs of his hand and wrists. He had wanted kids, at one point saw himself with a houseful of children, at least three or four, all the noise and work and chaos of children running wild up and down stairs, through the house and backyard, taking over his life with hugs and kisses and the miracle of small life born mysteriously through his. He had wanted a wife, mother of his children, person who knew him inside and out, accepted his faults, supported his dreams.

Nia waited for him to answer, smiling like everything he had ever wanted possible, like he was going to live forever and he had yet to tell her otherwise.

He forced clenched muscles to relax, viciously fought off the beginnings of a migraine.

"Yeah, I guess I want children."

She reached over with a napkin, wiped cold, messy ice cream from his flushed skin.

"You're dripping. You've never thought about having children?"

He licked at butter pecan cone, sweetness of the ice cream tart and bitter against his tongue.

"No, not recently."

"I want as many as I can have. Let me take that back. I want as many as I can afford."

She wanted children. She was down to just her cone, ice cream all gone and she nibbled at the cone slowly, tried to make it last.

He didn't want to think about the things he couldn't give her, things she had every right to expect from a man. He didn't know how to tell her that no healthy whole children possible from his diseased and damaged seed. The remainder of his life, weeks or months or years, depending on how

fast the virus able to conquer and subdue his immune system, stretched out like acres and acres of polluted soil where
nothing worth having, nothing anyone needed able to flour-
ish, grow.

He smiled a good-bye smile that she failed to notice.

"You'll have all the children you want, more than you
can probably handle. You just wait."

She finished her cone, wiped her mouth and hands,
raised her hands over her head, up to the heavens.

"That's what I'm doing. Just waiting."

There was no way for him to finish ice cream, a deep
freeze settled in skin and flesh and bones to stay indefinitely.
All his desperate pretending was over and done.

He threw the last of his ice cream in the trash close to
their table.

"You ready to go?"

"Yes, I'm ready."

He walked her home, kissed her quick on the cheek,
afraid to even touch her because he was no longer pretending and simple touch maybe enough to leave her rotten inside as well.

He never saw her again, stranded lonely in the middle of
his polluted life.

Chapter Seventeen

The boys in Eden were in grave danger of staying boys forever, standing on street corners, huddled on front porches, eyes glazed with pleasant childhood dreams of wealth and plenty without work, without effort, without desire. They waited for all the good things in life to fall from green tree branches overhead, to drip like stale water from a leaking roof. They pissed on the rim and around the floor of clean toilet seats, left dirty dishes in the sink day and night until food crusted over and dishes impossible to clean, threw dirty clothes haphazardly all about the house, left shit-stained boxers and briefs on the bathroom floor, soaking in the bathroom sink. Red Cap walked through town, his fishing rod thrown easy over his shoulder, and thought about boys in danger of staying boys forever, fascinated, appalled.

His breakfast of bacon, eggs, grits, and biscuits sat heavy in his gut. Early day summer breeze was warm and insistent against his face. He thought about boys in danger of being boys forever in supermarkets with their wives, girlfriends, mamas, pulling at skirts, begging for candy, sweet cereal, chocolate-chip cookies, a few extra dollars for beer or weed. Wives, girlfriends, mamas looked harassed, beaten down, sighed and put too-sweet cereal or cookies in shopping carts, reluctantly handed over five and ten dollar bills, anything to get the hands of boys forever in danger of staying boys off them.

Most of them were grown, at least eighteen, and living on the backs of women, treating women like disposable income and the women so grateful to have anyone at all that that they hoarded the little bit of love and kindness thrown carelessly, tried not to think about how little they actually received.

There were already men on the corner. Men with no jobs, no hobbies, no interests. Most of them he knew. They waved at him, nodded heads.

"How you doing, Mr. Red?"

He nodded back at them, wondered how they withstood the pressure of useless days strung together one after the other.

"I'm fine. You all hanging in there?"

They laughed like he was hopelessly dated, unforgivably old.

"Oh, yeah. We hanging in there, still fighting the good fight."

"Yeah, well . . ."

One of the men, Louie, tall and dark with dead eyes asked, "Heard Jeremiah coming home. That true?"

"Yeah. Should be in this morning."

Louie picked at his fingernails with a toothpick lifted from behind his ear.

"You tell him hey for me."

"Okay."

Red turned away from them, paused when he heard a coughed "Jeremiah a faggot" at his back.

They all laughed, that one sentence the extent of their amusement for the day.

Red kept walking, heard their laughter, imagined them rolling eyes and sucking teeth at his back. He wanted to sit them down and tell them some things and felt a harsh blush along his cheeks because he wasn't sure if he knew anything worth telling. Jeremiah was coming home sick, all of Eden knew it, and men in danger of being boys forever stupidly taking pleasure in another person's pain. He didn't understand them, tried hard to forgive them their ignorance, their lack of any kind of ambition, and any kind of pride.

He wasn't like boys in danger of being boys forever, didn't live off women, didn't expect women to give him portions of small paychecks Friday evenings. He always worked, always had his own place. He didn't move back home once he was grown until after Mama and Daddy died and no one but him left to tend the house in his family since before the Civil War.

He liked women, loved the softness and the way women were more comfortable in their skin than men, more ready to laugh or cry, not all the time shutting off emotions. Before the Korean War, before he went to watch bodies blown from the face of the earth, grown men vanish leaving nothing but neon streaks of blood behind, he thought that he'd marry. That's what men in his generation did, fought for home and country, married some pretty young girl, had enough babies to overrun a big old house.

War changed him, the futility of responsibility and doing what needed to be done proven by acres and acres of men with body parts gone, legs and toes and fingers and feet. Men sent home with useless arms or hands, men sent home never able to walk again, men never sent home at all. The sight of rapidly fired bullets buzzing in the air like millions and millions of fireflies or shooting stars had astounded him, stayed with him long after he returned to the States. Even now he had dreams of night skies on fire, the choking, hoarse screams of wounded or dying men.

When he came home from war he was ready to play, no thoughts at all of wife and kids and happily ever after. Wife and kids were responsibility and doing what needed to be done. He had known men during the war now dead with families waiting at home. A wife and kids no protection against bad things happening, no springboard into eternal life.

Eden was slow to life in the mornings. It was still too early for children to be waiting on school buses to take them to summer camps. There were no children in front yards playing mother-may-I and green light–red light on grass browned by the scorching sun. There were no old people sitting in comfortable porch chairs, enjoying watching children play, lightly fanning themselves with folded pieces of newspaper, and sipping on ice-cold lemonade, iced tea, or beer.

Red kept walking, thought about all the women he had held, touched, loved since coming back from the Korean War. Beautiful women with soft eyes and thighs, high breasts, smooth-as-stone skin. Kind women who fixed and served him dinner at their tables, let him sleep in their beds, helped buy and wash his clothes because they felt sorry for a man all alone, a man with no woman of his own to take care of him. They understood that he, for whatever reasons, didn't want tuxedos and white dresses, didn't want to set up house, didn't want children. All the things he didn't want were enough to turn some women bitter if Red wasn't so considerate. He remembered birthdays and first dates and special places. Red played well with children not his, especially boys, took them to movies and parks and play-grounds and fishing at the lake. Red was a friend, a good friend, long after sex ended. He loaned money for rent, to help children get ready for the new school year, or to help teenagers off to college, and never mentioned it again.

Red didn't realize, until he was well into his fifties, that nothing in the world worth anything was his. Women he used to run with were married and settled down or occupied with grandchildren and girlfriends and church, relieved to be finally done with men. Children he used to help care for had families and children of their own, no time at all to visit an old man.

He knew Vern, had known her all her life the way peo-ple in small towns familiar with each other. He always thought she was a pretty thing, but she was quite a few years younger and married almost before she turned eight-een to some horn player from New York. He liked her first husband, used to hang out with him drinking and smoking Friday through Sunday. Her first husband easy to laugh, quick to tell jokes, pleasant to be around, and Red recog-nized in him the same aversion that he had to responsibility, to being any woman's all and everything. He had known, like everyone in town, that they weren't going to make it for the long haul; no twenty-fifth and fortieth anniversaries loomed pleasantly in their future. He was surprised the mar-riage lasted for almost ten years with her first husband out at the speakeasies or down at the jazz clubs in Cleveland playing and listening to music more than he was home.

After her first husband was gone, Vern spent all her time and energy on her sons. She didn't date really, never had no man spend the night at her place when her kids were little as far as he knew. She was Mama. Sometimes Red ran into her at the bank or grocery store and she always looked tired, always looked not quite done, as if she had little or no time for herself. Red always felt sorry for her. He always wondered how she managed to pack away, store indefinitely everything she ever wanted to do or be before children. Sometimes they talked, simple conversations that usually focused on her boys. Boys growing up quick, turning into men, at any day and time ready to leave her. When all her boys were grown, the oldest dead, and the other two living their lives, he saw the weight of an empty house about her shoulders. Red looked at her and knew she was as lonely as he.

His loneliness snuck up on him, he didn't realize in the middle of his no responsibility and endless good time that growing old was sometimes sad. Sometimes completely isolating especially with no wife, children, or grandchildren, no blood kin.

He started courting Vern. Followed her to the grocery and the post office Saturday mornings, listened for the surprised startle of her laughter, loved the way she laughed so hard her entire body wiggled, thrown completely off balance. For the first time he looked at a woman, and allowed himself to feel more than the expectation of simple sex with nothing after. Simple sex with no accountability other than being, and not necessarily all the time, halfway kind and decent. He rediscovered part of himself he thought stranded into immobility by quick-buzzing bullets and planes blown up like meteors in the sky. He still had the same dreams, still wanted a wife and children and house full of people who belonged to him.

He cornered Vern at the post office one Saturday morning, and waited for her.

Vern came out of the post office, stopped in her tracks when she saw him leaning against the cab of his truck.

"Hey, Red."

"How you doing, Vern?"

"I'm good. You?"

"No complaints at all."

She looked up and down the street, puzzled.

"Who you waiting on?"

"You."

She laughed, quick, startled laugh.

"Pardon me?"

"I know you heard me, Vern. I'm waiting on you."

Her laughter gone that quick, and she considered him. He knew she was thinking about an empty house and no one to go home for.

"Oh."

"Can I give you a ride?"

"You know what, Red? I'd like that."

They were married within six months and he was amazed at how much he was able to love once a concrete decision was made. Love was not possible for him at all until he choose it. Now he had her children and a granddaughter and he felt like he was the luckiest man walking through Eden, his grandbaby, Lula, the brightest, cutest thing ever born.

Jeremiah was coming home today and he knew that Vern needed him with her. He remembered Jeremiah as a boy the way that Eden remembered the childhoods of all its children. Jeremiah was a fine child, capable of long moments of silence, long howls of laughter. He was the child old women sent to the store and old men took with them to speakeasies and poker games. And he was Vern's baby and there was nothing that she could do, that anyone could do to keep him safe and whole.

Red considered walking through Eden on the way to the lake his exercise, a means of steadying himself for what was surely coming. He wasn't that old, still got around. Although Vern fussed over him like he was a child, telling him no talking to strangers or getting into cars, like he had absolutely no sense.

He saw his neighbor, Eddie, sitting on his front porch, sipping coffee.

"Hey, Eddie. What you doing up this time of day?"

"Red? That you? Bring your black ass on up here."

Red laughed, and joined Eddie on the porch.

"How you been?" Eddie sipped slow at steaming coffee.

"Can't complain. Can't complain. I like these chairs, Eddie."

"I know. Tell you a secret, my wife got them from Sears, and they ain't cost all that much."

"How's your wife?"

"She's all right. In there lying down. Those hoodlum grandkids were here last night. Wore her out."

"How many you got again?"

"Six and counting."

"How are they?"

"Bad. They are bad. What about yours?"

"Man, she's too young to be bad. She's just over a year."

"They're cute at that age, aren't they?"

"Yeah, they are. She's all the time grinning at me. Like I was the best thing in the world."

"You wait until she gets three and starts talking back and telling you what she ain't going to do."

"You know you love them."

"I do. They're bad, but they're mine. Where you headed, anyway?"

"To the lake, going to do a little fishing before the day gets started good."

"I heard Jeremiah coming home."

"He'll get in a little later this morning."

"You know you all are in our prayers."

"I sincerely thank you for that, Eddie."

They were quiet for a moment, staring out at a mostly sleeping Eden.

Eddie cleared his throat, shifted slightly in his chair.

"You know I don't go to church, regularly. But I read something in one of my wife's daily prayer books. It went something like, 'There is no burden love can't bear, no sin love won't pardon, and no suffering the Lord can't heal.' "

"I'll keep that in mind."

"It's just something . . . It helps me sometimes."

"Listen, let me get down to the lake before all the fish head up to Canada."

"You take it easy."

"I'll try."

"All you got to do is call if you need something, man."

"I will, Eddie. I will. Catch you later."

"You be careful out here."

"You sound like Vern."

Red tried to think good thoughts and Lula's small face came to mind. Lula was soft and sweet smelling and all around precious. He had missed babies, too caught up with all kinds of women and simple pleasures. Now nothing to distract him from loving Lula, he held her, sang to her, rocked her to sleep, took her on walks and cradled her against his chest.

There was a dead cat in the road before him, flesh and fur turned inside out and outside in. He stood still for a moment, fascinated by the maze of tissue and organ. He felt fear hot and salty in his mouth, wondered if love was enough the way Eddie seemed to think, and prayed hard that it was.

Chapter Eighteen

Hawk Eye ran up and down Appletree Street like cars and slow-lumbering public transportation buses didn't exist, like he wasn't flesh and blood at all, in no danger of bones crushing and breaking, cars and buses dragging him for blocks. Every early summer morning Hawk Eye was up with children in shorts and T-shirts waiting for big yellow buses to go to day camp and men and women with too many clothes on. Men and women sullen with heat rising from the ground, and the day not even started yet, on their way to work.

The children laughed at him, nibbled on fried-egg sandwiches, sipped juice from brightly colored box cartons. Huge eyes watched Hawk Eye day in and day out all summer long. Hawk Eye knew they were fascinated, knew they wanted to ask him how and why was he in the streets, just running up and down, and they had to wait for red lights and firm adult hands. Children were well groomed, smelling like decent homes, eyebrows and cheeks shiny with their mama's spit. They were too polite to do anything but laugh into their juice boxes, choke on fried eggs creamy with butter.

Appletree Street was no small side street with cars lined up on one side with just a hint of sidewalk in front of homes. Appletree was a large, two way street, cars coming from both directions, buses leaving thick black smoke long after they passed. Buses rode down Appletree Street wearily to the bus depot at the very end of the street, the very end of the world, where Appletree dropped into a long stretch of highway and quietly disappeared. He raced back-and-forth between sidewalks. Sidewalks defined the corners and edges of his existence the same way stones thrown randomly at numbers dictated how far children could jump during hopscotch. He dashed out from behind parked cars to loud horns and cursing, his smile wide and easy, enjoying his game because he was as good as untouchable. Nothing in Eden able to do him any kind of harm without him seeing it coming first. He was almost invincible and invincibility boring day in and day out if he didn't mock it just a little bit, take a few unhealthy risks.

Women and men in town stared at him like he was sick, out of his head, pitiful. He ran out in front of their cars, startling them, and sometimes they swerved cars politely from his path, sometimes they pressed their foot just a little harder on the gas to scare some sense into him. Sometimes drivers stopped, got out the car to talk to him. Women with hair permed straight or done in long braids and twisted up. Voices hounded at him as he ran away from the scene.

"Hawk Eye, honey, you're going to get yourself killed out here. You need to stop it now before you seriously get hurt or hurt someone else. The last thing I want to see on my way home from work is your body squashed and flattened in the middle of Appletree Street. That's no kind of way to die, not even for a dog."

They spoke quietly and softly, but the hint of a threat was

just under their voice like mothers talked to children showing out in public. Hawk Eye got away from them as fast as he could.

The men were not as nice, they always pressed their foot on the gas like Hawk Eye was a stray cat or slow-moving squirrel too stupid to live. They hollered at him from windows.

"You one fucked up individual, man. You know that?"

Hawk Eye knew men were furious because he in know way resembled at all what a man should be or do or want in life. He didn't have no job, no place, no woman, no responsibilities. He was just in the world taking up valuable space, making all black men look irresponsible and crazy. There were exceptions, of course. Red Cap was always nice to him because Red used to date Mama after Daddy left, used to spend nights in Mama's bed and wake him up in the mornings to fix his breakfast and get him ready for school. Red took him fishing on the weekends at Lake Erie, made sure that he always had new clothes and shoes, always had a few extra dollars in his pockets for any expenses that might unexpectedly pop up for an eleven-year-old boy. Red Cap, he knew, loved him almost like a son and Hawk Eye watched Red's face go slack with sorrow and pity each and every time they ran into each other, which was at least once a day. Eden was not the kind of place where avoiding someone possible.

Children on their way to summer camp early mornings ate fried-egg sandwiches and sipped juice and just stared. The boldest, some child always well dressed and well taken care of and certain of their worth, shouted politely at him.

"Mr. Hawk Eye? Hey! Mr. Hawk Eye, why you going to go and do something like that?"

He hollered back at them if he was across the street, talked in normal tones if they shared the same sidewalk.

"Don't you worry nothing about it. What I'm doing, this here is grown folks business."

Hawk Eye knew they didn't believe him, just laughed some more into their sandwiches, sipped harder, longer at their juice boxes. Children with shiny dark faces and no fear in the eyes or riding about the mouth, pinching lips and leaving the insides of cheeks bloody with teeth marks. Their skin smelled like baby lotion and their flesh was plump and sometimes Hawk Eye just wanted to eat them up. They looked that good, smelled that clean and yummy.

Hawk Eye stared at children's smug faces, sure and cocky smiles. He wanted to tell them, wanted to pull them aside, sit them on the sidewalk curb and be the first one to whisper it in their ear, the first one to run fingers over gorgeous child-smooth skin, kinky oiled hair. He wanted to tell them child-smooth hands and kinky oiled hair wasn't forever, tell them there was no promise anyone would be running around alive and busy from one moment to the next. Something hungry and vicious and sometimes kind and always surprising was constantly nipping at heels, tripping up feet.

He knew it intimately, knew the something always following everyone around—to work and back, snuggled up in bed, sitting spread out and comfortable on the couch. Women knew the smell of it, he wasn't sure why, but watching Mama taught him women knew lots of things that men didn't get most of the time; when a child was hurt or scared, when to hold tongues and when to let tongues race and scorch and do real damage. Women got up from their beds in the middle of the night to check on lovers and children like fixing covers and kissing small cheeks and hands might make some kind of difference. Hawk Eye knew it was out of their hands, knew they knew it was out of their hands.

Hadn't he seen it coming, spread out on the sterile bed in

the emergency room of Eden hospital five years ago? Doctors poking and prodding at him, trying to stop the blood sucked from under his skin like water going slowly, inevitably down a drain by cuts so deep that some spots showed bone. He saw it coming for him, laid out, every part of him hurting, skid marks from where the car dragged him before coming to a complete stop racing up and down his body, clothes ripped and torn. Some people called it death, but Hawk Eye knew death too small a word, not even a pretty sounding word. He saw it strolling, rushing along like some kind of storm, but cool and easy and calm like days from his childhood sitting on the steps with Mama late afternoon and the wind like his mama's fingers over his face. It didn't look like no death, looked like Lady Day to him, all that sweetness and something so ferocious, so awful that there was no running, just sitting and waiting still for whatever Lady Day wanted to do.

Hawk Eye waited for Lady Day on that hospital bed soaked with his blood, watched Lady Day kind of dance and sway toward him, back off a bit, teasing. He was relaxing, pain easing, and enjoying Lady Day's coquettishness when Lady Day slowly backed off, taking the sweetness and easy calm. The pain came back like large thumbs digging into bloody flesh, scraping at bones.

Doctors patched him up and sent him home to Mama. He was good and grown and still living in the back room of Mama's house, still letting Mama cook dinner and wash clothes and clean for him. His room was painted dark green and cream carpet covered the floor and everything neat and in its place. Hawk Eye took his time getting well, wasn't no reason to go down and get breakfast or lunch or dinner because Mama brought it up. Mama made sure he had daily newspapers and weekly news magazines and hot coffee and clean bedding and underwear. Wasn't until he left the house, took his first step outside and felt sun like something soft and melting all down his face that he saw Lady Day. Saw Lady Day just walking up and down the street with people, dancing with them the way Lady Day danced with him in the hospital. Saw Lady Day being calm and sweet and saw Lady Day being ugly. Lady Day came and grabbed up people, danced and rocked away with people. Seduced them like lover's hands in the middle of the night. Surprised them like stick-up boys with loaded guns sneaking up from Cleveland jumping out from slowly moving cars with tinted windows.

Hawk Eye was so amazed he started telling people. Not lots of people, just a body hear and there. He went to the convenience store to buy a pack of cigarettes and a Coke and saw Lady Day dancing up real hard on old man Grey, who owned the corner store,

He tried to tell old man Grey.

"I see Lady Day coming for you and, man, you better move your ass."

Old man Grey looked up and down crowded aisles.

"Who the hell is Lady Day, man?"

"Death. Just death."

Old man Grey sucked his teeth, rolled his eyes.

"Yeah. Okay. You're out your head. That car didn't drag you far enough."

Mrs. Horter from around the corner was in the store buying bread and milk for her kids, Mr. Green waited in line behind Hawk Eye to buy the day's paper, teenage boys stood in front of the open doorway sipping at pineapple pop and chewing bubble gum. They all laughed.

Hawk Eye knew what he knew and he saw what he saw. Two days later old man Grey was found dead on his stool behind the cash register, heart split down the middle like an animal's innards by somebody's knife-wielding child. The child didn't even get much money, a few twenties and all of them stained with old man Grey's blood when the police found him playing craps alongside an abandoned house in Cleveland.

Lady Day shaking her ass all through Eden like Eden the best good time reminded Hawk Eye of Uncle Willie. Uncle Willie long since dead, but when he was a little boy, Uncle Willie, his missing-in-action-Daddy's-brother, ate turtles. Hawk Eye watched Uncle Willie kill lazy turtles he caught in the stream behind the high school and make turtle stew. The turtles stupid and frightened in their shells until Uncle Willie took a huge rock and cracked the shell open. The body bare and vulnerable, looked like something sickly or something half cooked. Hawk Eye wanted to pick it up and hold it close to the bare flesh under his shirt.

He shook his head at Uncle Willie the way children quick to shake their heads at cruelty.

"You can't buy that at the supermarket?"

He was thinking about going to the supermarket with Mama around Thanksgiving and Christmas. Thanksgiving and Christmas and the supermarkets stocked with chitterlings, pig's feet, cow's tongue, tripe and all kinds of things Hawk Eye didn't think belonged on anyone's plate. Supermarkets carried all that so why not frozen and nicely diced turtle so he didn't have to stand in Uncle Willie's backyard in midday with the sun sitting like a large stack of books on his head, eating at the long length of his bare legs and watch Uncle Willie kill an already mostly dead thing.

Uncle Willie laughed at him, laughed until his cream brown cheeks were red and puffed out like an old Santa Claus trying to blow out matches or candles. His laughter light and sweet, there was nothing at all mean about Uncle Willie except his hands tightening around the turtle's throat, efficient and nonchalant.

He stopped telling people about Lady Day; no point to it at all, folks believed what they wanted to believe. Any kind of heads up or warning he might give nothing more than a joke. He knew all of Eden thought he was crazy until somebody died suddenly and they tried to remember if he had said something, done something, followed the soon-to-be-dead person around offering last good-byes and bidding safe journey. He knew there had to be The Other Side. The mere fact that Lady Day strolled up and down streets, wandered in and out of homes and hospitals and cars a kind of undeniable proof. Hawk Eye didn't believe in God really until he saw Lady Day. He used to go to church and pray at night, but there was no sincerity in any of his actions, he was just going through motions because Mama wanted him to have some kind of relationship with the Lord. He lived under her roof so what else was there for him to do? After he saw the confidence and viciousness of Lady Day, he knew there had to be a God, strength and salvation, because without that there was no way and no reason at all to endure.

He had known it yesterday when he walked through the valley death, Lady Day on his shoulder the entire morning as he headed to the mall construction site along the highway. Lady Day so close to him, closer even than when he was in the hospital after the car dragged him down Appletree Street and his blood quick to soak sterile, white sheets. He woke up yesterday morning and Lady Day sat at the foot of his bed, like a cat or small dog curled up but nothing at all friendly or safe about Lady Day. He stayed still in bed, closed his eyes, thought good thoughts—ice cream on hot summer days, fresh baked bread still warm from the oven, big weekend breakfasts, the way the sky looked in late afternoons once thunderstorms passed, the last time he saw Daddy before he left for places unknown. Mama told him to think good thoughts when he had nightmares as a child and consistently wet the bed because he was too scared of things in the dark to put bare feet on the floor and take the long walk to the toilet. Mama assured him good thoughts made bad things disappear.

Hawk Eye opened tightly closed eyes, saw bright yellow dots skip along ceilings and walls and the dark blue of his bedspread, saw Lady Day still curled at the foot of the bed, waiting on him. He got up quick, rushed to the bathroom, hid in the shower, warm water stinging his face and chest. Lady Day was behind him, lazily soaping his back and all his insides froze, his lips lost all color, and some strands of his hair went completely gray. He aged a good five years in the shower, standing under warm, pleasant water. He thought that he was invulnerable because he had enough time to sidestep and run hard and fast. He realized, while Lady Day lazily and thoroughly soaped his back, that there was no escape from inevitability, the fall from Eden and ashes to ashes and dust to dust.

He left the shower and got dressed. Lady Day handed him shorts and shirts and socks and shoes. He didn't eat breakfast, just left the house. Mama sat at the kitchen table alone, sipping tea and he smiled at her, didn't want her to see that everything inside him good as dead with terror. Outside the heat vigilant and determined, sweat poured down his back and chest, under his arms, as soon as he felt sun on his face. He walked along Appletree Street, walked along the highway to the construction site where Red Cap and lots of other men from Eden worked, Lady Day heavy and patient on his shoulders. He didn't want Lady Day to take him anywhere near Mama, didn't want Mama to see his battered and lifeless body balled up like useless papers thrown in the trash.

He saw Red Cap pass by in his truck, looked like Pete in the passenger seat. He saluted them because he knew this was a death march, a funeral procession, and saluting seemed more formal than a wave, lent the whole thing some dignity even though he was soaked with sweat. There was dirt blown from the highway by fast-moving cars in his hair and eyes, like sand in his mouth.

Hawk Eye reached the construction site shortly after noon and men looked at him from patches of shade, from over their lunches like he was good and crazy and he wanted to cry because he wished he were—wished he was just hallucinating and Lady Day not tugging like a child at his short Afro. Men made space for him under small patches of shade, shared their lunches and juices and sodas. He didn't remember what he ate, didn't remember what they talked about, and he knew they must have talked because that's what black men did when they got together. He didn't remember anything but the car coming dead at him full speed. He didn't move because Lady Day had a tight hold around his throat. His head was empty except for Psalms 23:6:

> Surely goodness and mercy shall follow me all the days of my life: and I will dwell in the house of the Lord forever.

Lady Day jumped real graceful from his shoulders when the car was almost upon him. The car turned slow, just missed him, and came to a hard stop in the grass along the highway by the construction site. He didn't stay around long, told everyone he was fine, wiggled all ten fingers and toes, and went home.

That was yesterday and this morning he was up early like always, wandering Appletree Street like his entire world the length and width of the long stretch of coal black tar. He knew his role in life was undeniably limited, nothing more than a vigilant watchdog against Lady Day. He was kinder to people when he knew Lady Day was on the way for them. He watched them with pity, spoke to them in soft tones, made sure to be there at the final moment just so they had a face to focus on instead of terror. That was only when he was feeling invulnerable, like Lady Day had no right to touch him when he knew deep in the bone that his life belonged to Lady Day straight from the cradle. When he allowed himself to acknowledge that all roads led to Lady Day he hid under beds, didn't leave his house, stayed away from Appletree Street entirely. Lady Day all the time smiling and waving at him far too much to handle day in and day out.

Hawk Eye sat on the curb of Appletree Street, across from the bus station, and watched the first Greyhound bus of the morning pull in. The Greyhound bus came in and dark clouds and soft rain followed, gradually sucked startling heat from air. There was a sudden cooling breeze against his skin. He didn't mind the rain, opened his mouth and tilted his head back and soft rain fell light against his tongue, the length and width of his face. People limped from the bus, exhausted from the long trip. The women in wrinkled slacks and shirts, wilted like all gardens in Eden from the heat. The children stretched to the sky, slapped lightly at arms and legs to make sure body parts were still there. The few teenagers had hair all over the head and earphones on, heads nodding to a beat unheard by anyone else.

A man walked slow down the steep steps of the bus, took a minute to steady himself once his feet on solid ground. He was well dressed but too thin. Clothes hung from his frame, his eyes and mouth too big for his face.

Hawk Eye recognized Jeremiah in the man's thin face and deep eyes. Jeremiah used to be his best friend and was always nice to him when he came home even though everyone else in Eden treated him like he needed help in the worst way. He and Jeremiah were the same age. He used to play with Jeremiah and Aspasia when they were children—climbing trees, fighting wars in the green surrounding town, riding bikes all through Eden. He still remembered the summer day when they found the unimaginable hidden in the green surrounding town, the day that all but ended their friendship and changed their lives forever. The day was like falling from the edges of the world into deep, dark space. After that summer day they avoided each other in the streets, at school, in the playground.

Hawk Eye smiled at Jeremiah, about to get up, when Lady Day peeked at him from behind Jeremiah's expensive button-down shirt. Lady Day was riding Jeremiah's shoulders, playing with Jeremiah's hair, gently kissing the back of Jeremiah's neck. Lady Day forced Hawk Eye to sit back down, hold his head in hands, and look down at cracks and crevices hidden in cement sidewalks. He knew nothing was forever, nothing permanent, but he sometimes forgot and Lady Day always insisted on reminding him. He didn't want to face Jeremiah, not with Lady Day already laying claim to his thin and fragile body.

Hawk Eye got up, went home, curled himself underneath his bed, didn't leave the house for the rest of the day.

Chapter Nineteen

The rain followed Jeremiah all the way to Eden, and broke an almost three-month heat wave. Flowers and grass and lakes, desperate and thirsty for water, were relieved. Jeremiah got off the bus and still tasted heat in the air, still felt heat on his face, but soft rain gently cooled things down. He looked up and down the street, saw front yards wilted and dry and hungry for rain. He watched as grass regained some color and flowers made determined attempts to stand upright instead of wilting to the side. Birds were in the air above him, birds flying in mad circles, around and around, feathered wings glossy with wet. He never saw birds flying in the rain before. They told him just how bad a summer it was, just how thirsty and desperate every living thing was.

The butter and sugar smell from the Sweet Cake factory assaulted his senses, made eyes and mouth water. The butter and sugar smell called up hunger deep inside him and he wanted to bend down, gather up Eden's dirt, shove fistfuls into his mouth.

It was still early, sun just up in the sky and Eden quiet, no one on the roads or in the streets just yet. He was the only passenger from the bus staying in Eden, everyone else just getting off to stretch their legs or smoke cigarettes. Eden was not the kind of place circled on any tourist's map. The bus driver unloaded Jeremiah's bags, placed them at his side. The other passengers got back in the bus, gave him tentative smiles and shy waves. The Greyhound bus heaved into motion, stuttered onto the street headed for the highway, going west. He watched the bus until it was gone, sat down on his bags, waited. He had told Pete what time he was getting in, but he knew neither Pete nor Mama was going to meet him. He waited on who was coming like his whole life nothing more than preparation for this exact moment in time. He was waiting so hard and with such concentration that he didn't notice Hawk Eye across the street until Hawk Eye walked away from him. He only knew it was Hawk Eye because every now and then Hawk Eye turned back to look at him and shake his head. Jeremiah had seen that kind of headshake before, the kind of shake men gave when nothing they could do because their hands were tied.

He watched Hawk Eye go, looked up at gray skies and soft-falling rain. In every movie he'd ever seen, every book he'd ever read, rain not a good sign of things to come.

There was no way for Jeremiah to know that women woke from their sleep in tears as soon as his feet touched down gently on Eden's soil. Women still in beds next to husbands and lovers woke up crying from lightness in the breast—sweet, innocent ache for girls they were and boys they used to love. They woke up in tears desperately missing grandmas and great-grandmas and mamas long since dead in the grave. Women in Eden overtaken by sweet, bitter ache brought to life by rain tapping at windows and rooftops, and Jeremiah's feet on Eden's soil.

Jeremiah sat on the hard fullness of his bags, watched Hawk Eye until Hawk Eye was no longer in sight. Hawk Eye and Aspasia were with him when the earth vanished from under his feet for the very first time—the first long, unsafe leap into adulthood and nothing ever the same. He still remembered that long-ago summer day when they went exploring in the green around Eden. The green was made for children's imaginations. On any given day green might be jungles, tropical forests, swamps, deep blue oceans, or castles and fortresses magically formed beneath hanging tree branches. Hawk Eye wasn't Hawk Eye then, he was just Keith, and they were all children running through the green with invisible bandits quick on their heels, invisible warm breath hot against the back of their necks. They had long sticks for sharp swords in their hands, carried close to their waists. Shirts tucked into the waistband of shorts, dingy white headbands around their temples, catching their sweat. Brown skin of their faces and legs and arms glowed deep red and yellow from summer sun, flesh scarce because all of them always running about, unable to keep weight on, muscles lean and pronounced.

They ran, screaming through the green, holding their sides and laughing because the sun on their faces and leaves overhead and grass underfoot and their young bodies strong and sure. Their legs carried them wherever they wanted, arms moved in rhythm with racing feet, hands held tight to long sticks used for sharp swords.

They stopped when they were sure invisible bandits no longer gave chase, when they were too tired and too out of breath to run any more. They all sat beneath large tall tree, rested their backs against rough tree bark. They didn't mind ants crawling up and down legs and arms, didn't mind ladybugs landing on their foreheads and in their hair, didn't mind bees insistently buzzing. They sat comfortable, used long sticks for swords to dig deep in the earth, watched worms and all sorts of pale, rubbery insects scramble to get out of the way, avoid being crushed.

Jeremiah's stick reached something solid and smooth first. He thought it was rock until he saw bright whiteness almost bare in the earth. Bright whiteness looked like linoleum floors cleaned with bleach, cold and sterile.

Whiteness scared him and he spoke to Keith and Aspasia in soft tones.

"Hey. Look at this."

They leaned over him, stared at whiteness surrounded by deep, black earth.

Aspasia reached out carefully to touch. She stilled her hand just above the whiteness, pulled it away, guarded it in her lap.

"What is it?"

Jeremiah shook his head.

"I don't know. Thought you all might know."

Keith's eyes were bright, no uneasiness settling in his stomach the way it had in Jeremiah's.

"Nope. You think we should try and get it out?"

Jeremiah didn't want to move it, didn't want to touch it at all, but Keith and Aspasia were already looking for a big sturdy stick to dig whiteness out from ground.

"I don't know if we should mess with it like that."

Aspasia stared at Jeremiah, disappointed in his lack of courage.

"Why not?"

Jeremiah told himself that her disappointment didn't matter as much as the sick feeling in his gut.

"I don't know. I just don't think we should."

Keith slapped him lightly on the back of the head, and he felt the sweat from Keith's palm leave an imprint on the flesh beneath his hair.

"Man, stop being a pussy and help us get it out."

"I'm not no pussy."

Aspasia was quick to smooth things over.

"All right, so help us dig."

They dug around whiteness, careful not to scrape sticks against the smooth surface. They dug and dug, ignoring insects and heat and sun melting on their faces. They created a small deep hole, piles of dirt on either side. The day slowly passed like summer days last forever for children. They kept digging. The piles of dirt on either side of the hole grew thicker and higher, covering summer green grass and bright wildflowers. The whiteness was neverending, bones and more bones, shining white like cold milk poured into a fresh, clean glass. Childhood fascinations with death kept them digging even though for each of them death was something that happened somewhere else to some other people. Jeremiah wanted to stop, his hands tired and the stick he used to dig on the verge of breaking from constant motion.

The dirt smelled good, smelled like every summer that they'd ever experienced, smelled like the hair of all the women who lived in Eden, smelled like the hands of all the men.

They stopped digging, realized that the whiteness might go on forever, go way deep, past the soil and the firmament, all the way down to the Hell and Damnation that the Reverend Tinsley was always preaching about in Church early Sunday mornings.

They took a small piece of whiteness out of the deep black earth, stared at it for a long time. The green made for children's imaginations was absolutely still around them—no birds and no breeze and no scurrying feet and even the insects quiet.

Jeremiah shook his head, tears wet in eyes and throat burning.

"This can't be what I think it is. I know it can't be that."

Keith touched whiteness, ran fingers, hesitant and gentle, over its long length.

"I think it is, Jeremiah. I think this one's, what do you call it? The one in your thigh?"

Jeremiah cleared his throat, hoped he didn't cry because then he'd really be a pussy.

"I don't know."

Aspasia pounded the heel of her hand against her forehead

"Why can't I remember what the one in the thigh is called?"

Jeremiah forced himself to touch smooth, slightly ridged whiteness.

"It's a femur. It's called a femur."

Keith pulled his fingers away, stared at them all with the first beginnings of horror riding his face.

"Yeah, you right. That's exactly what it is. Look at all these bones. I thought they might belong to cats or dogs, something like that. But they don't."

Aspasia stared down into the hole, stared down into bones mixed up and turned around, from the mess tried to imagine whole skeletons like the kind that were in all the science labs at school.

"I saw something like this on PBS. Me and Rachel were watching about slavery and how slaves were just dumped into big old graves. Just like this."

Bryan just shook his head at her.

"We ain't in the South. There wasn't no slavery in Ohio."

There were quick-racing ants like small holes shifting and moving over smooth whiteness. The ants seemed astonished to be scaling bones. Jeremiah brushed ants away, tried to keep the bones as spotless and pure as possible. He kept a steady fanning motion going just above the bones with both of his hands, watched ants carried away by air currents and the gentle touch of his fingers. It did little good because the hole was so deep and the bones piled on top of each other. Tree branches high overhead, leaves still lush and green, fall at least a month or so off. Sun and bright blue sky visible between leaves and branches, sun round and golden in the sky, sun scorching clouds like his heart on fire, lungs unable to suck in air.

Keith folded legs behind him, placed head in hands.

"Where did it all come from?"

Aspasia closed her eyes, reached out to the bones, left her fingers there for a moment, the slowly pulled her fingers away.

"I don't know."

Jeremiah fought the baby itch in his throat.

"I don't know either."

Keith was pulling absently at his hair with his hands. He pulled so tight that the skin around his hairline turned a dull red beneath the brown of his complexion.

"What you think we should do?"

Jeremiah just wanted to go home.

"I don't know."

Jeremiah stopped brushing ants off bone, let his hands and fingers wander across dark earth and bright green grass, thought about what else might be buried beneath the ground. The femur next to his hands just one bone in the human body and the human body had at least over a hundred. Jeremiah thought about missing bones beneath the ground, missing bones waiting to be found by children with strong and sturdy digging sticks.

Keith wanted to create a story for the bone, figure out who they belonged to and why it was waiting for them in earth.

"You remember anybody ever disappearing from Eden? Anybody police looking for or on them missing photos on the walls at the post office?"

Aspasia rolled her eyes.

"Keith, nobody ever disappears from Eden, you know that. And besides, look at all this. This is more than one person."

"Yeah, I know. But look, some people had to just vanish. We looking at bones and we ain't nowhere near the cemetery. They have to belong to somebody, they have to."

Jeremiah stared down at his hands moving through the piles of dirt on either side of the bones.

"They could have been here forever, man. Could have been out here for years and years and years, no way for us to know."

They went back to staring, tried not to think of all the things they didn't know, all the experiences waiting for them from now until their bones white and smooth in dark ground. They left their houses children, lifelong friends, headed for the green surrounding town to play. They weren't those children anymore, just strangers with death circling them.

Jeremiah sat facing his own mortality for the first time. His own mortality stared at him, stark and vivid, from wet green leaves overhead and full round bushes on all sides of him. He hadn't known death was an actual possibility in his life; certain he was going to live forever or at least as long as he wanted. Someday his own bones white and bare, stripped of skin and flesh and blood and buried in deep dark earth. He glanced at Keith and Aspasia, at the healthy tones of their dark brown skin, long length of their eyelashes, roundness of their cheeks and foreheads. Jeremiah was shaken to his very core because Keith and Aspasia's bare bones would eventually end up in deep dark earth too.

Jeremiah pulled his headband from off his head, double wrapped it around his wrist.

"I think we should leave them here."

Aspasia and Keith had no more words, they were just as scared, just as confused. They covered the hole with soil, bare mound of dark dirt looked defenseless in the middle of all that green.

They never mentioned the bones again, avoided each other for the rest of the summer.

An old Ford pulling into the Greyhound bus station startled Jeremiah from childhood memories. The car rumbled—like it was capable of falling all to pieces at any given moment—came to an easy stop not far from him. He wasn't at all surprised to see Eliza get out from behind the wheel. She was Eliza, healer and keeper of Eden like her mama and great-grandma and all firstborn girls sharing her blood and name before her. He was certainly in need of help, in need of make-all-better hands. Eliza was wearing a simple summer dress and soft rain shone in her hair, soft like dew on her skin. She was still pretty, still just as he remembered her when he used to play with Aspasia after school and on the weekends as a child.

She walked to him on long legs, smiled, took him instantly into her arms.

"How you doing, Jeremiah?"

He held onto her, the way he would hold onto Mama or Daddy or Pete, and knew he was home.

"I could be better, Eliza."

She pulled away from him, ran hands over his face.

"You look like you're holding your own."

He laughed.

"That's what I look like. Now, imagine how I actually feel."

She put his bags into the backseat of the car and he was too tired, too disoriented to help, only stood and watched.

She opened the passenger door for him.

"Let's get you home, baby."

He slid, grateful, into the front seat. Smokey Robinson played soft on the radio and the entire car smelled of Eliza's lavender water. Only women in Eden still wore simple floral waters. All the women in New York wore expensive, loud scents. Women in Eden were still able to appreciate subtleness, the power of the consistent and understated.

Eliza settled behind the wheel, handed him a scented cotton handkerchief to wipe soft rain from his face. She didn't bother with water on her own face, simply started the car.

"Look at you, Jeremiah. You went and brought the rain with you all the way from New York."

He smiled, shook his head.

"That's what I did?"

"That's what you did."

"I wish I had known something about it then. I was looking forward to feeling sun on my face, swimming down at the lake."

Eliza drove the car easily through empty streets.

"Don't worry, the sun coming back."

"I hope so."

She smiled at him, wide, effortless grin.

"It's coming, Jeremiah. I didn't realize it until the moment I came to get you and saw you standing there, and understood what you were bringing home with you."

"What have I brought home, Eliza? What do I have besides the clothes on my back?"

"Oh, sweet child of Eden. In you there is the possibility of redemption for us all."

Jeremiah turned away from her, stared out the window, tried to make her words make some kind of sense, but he was too tired to care.

They drove in silence, fog on the windows because her beat-up old Ford didn't have any air conditioner. She cracked the window on the driver side a little to get some air, not minding at all the slash of wet against her face.

"You in a hurry to get to Pete's and Aspasia's?"

He was in no rush to get anywhere at all, enjoying the ride and Eliza sitting next to him and the good smell of her lavender water.

"No, I have all the time you need."

"Okay. I want to take you someplace first. You mind getting a little wet?"

He laughed.

"I've been wet for months in New York, a little more won't kill me any faster. I know you know I'm dying."

The abrupt change of subject startled her for a brief moment. She glanced over at him.

"Yes. I know."

"Everyone in Eden know?"

"Yes. You know Eden. It's just a small town."

He stared out the window, recognized all the empty early morning streets, knew who lived in just about each house. Homecoming was nothing more than familiar places and people never forgotten, burned for all time into never-quite-fading memory. They were going to the green surrounding town, lush green where flowers and shrubs and grass and trees always growing, where earth rich and dark and good smelling, where his childhood lay scattered and discarded on soft wet grass.

Eliza parked the car, got out like there was no rain falling gentle from the sky, like the day hot and sunny instead of gray and overcast.

"You feel like walking?"

He remembered walking in the green with Daddy before Daddy left Eden and the entire state of Ohio for good; remembered running through the green with his brothers playing tag and hide-and-go-seek; remembered the summer day he discovered the unimaginable in deep dark earth with Keith and Aspasia.

"I can walk."

The earth soft and damp with rain, his feet sliding and slipping in his expensive shoes. He bent, took off shoes and socks, felt warm mud between his toes, and planted his feet more firmly in the ground. Eliza took off her sandals, carried them in one hand. They walked quiet until they came to a field where nothing grew except wildflowers.

The field held its breath, soft, damp earth hidden by vibrant wildflowers slightly wilted from the sun. Flowers knee high and he followed Eliza through flowers until they stood in the center of the clearing. Flowers smelled like all the summers he ever spent in Eden. The same flowers Mama and most of the women planted and nurtured in front gardens with the first melting of snow from the ground, the first hint of spring and ground pliable enough to be turned.

A huge wave of sadness overtook him, hundreds and hundreds of stones in his breast. Falling soft rain suddenly looked like tears and he held out his hands, wanting to wipe eyes and nose but nothing there. Lemon-yellow butter and sugar haze always over Eden washed clean momentarily, clouds in the sky and sky the murky blue color of old people's eyes. He knew he was standing in the middle of a holy place. Eliza was next to him, head bent in prayer and he knew she knew as well.

"Who's buried here, Eliza?"

Eliza reached down to pick wildflowers, held them lightly in her hand, spoke in hushed tones like she stood on sacred ground.

"Whole bunch of horror and pain."

"What happened here?"

Eliza shook her head, voice heavy and weakened.

"I think . . . I hope they've finally found some kind of peace. I hope we've all just found some small peace. We're just going to let them rest, okay?"

She grabbed his hand, cradled it in hers, pleaded with him with wide eyes. Jeremiah knew he had no right to break a secret kept since he was a child, no right to dig up bones.

"Okay."

The rain kept coming, dripped persistently from tree branches and overhanging leaves. The mud became softer and warmer, worms digging their way up from beneath earth, trying not to drown.

He only needed to ask her one more thing.

"Eliza? Eliza, you going to help me live?"

Helping him live had to be the reason she picked him up from the Greyhound bus station in her old beat-up Ford; helping him live the reason she brought him to the green, to this field. He was scared and so tired, felt his body becoming less and less his, each and everyday. He didn't know if he wanted her help, dreamed at night about fading away and no more pain, no more pills, no more doctors in white coats, his body no longer at war with itself.

Eliza let go of his hand, took him in her arms, arms surprisingly strong and smooth, fragrant with lavender. Her face was pleasant, her smile warm and reassuring.

"No, I'm going to help you die."

Jeremiah knew life eternal impossible for anyone, especially him; knew she didn't have all the answers, didn't know his final when and where and how, but she was going to be with him.

He grinned at her, relieved, and the soft rain fell all throughout Eden. Soft rain delivered the loud whisper of the Lord's voice. Powerful voices of the Lord, raging with majesty and redemption and all of Eden heard.

$\mathcal{A}$cknowledgments

My mother La-verne Helen Johnson and my grandmother, Annie Queen Johnson for raising me well

My husband, Dwayne Wharton for choosing me and standing beside me through all things

My brother, Keith Johnson and my uncle, Craig Johnson for silliness and laughter

Tori Johnson for being the little sister that I lost

Stephanie Lomax for giving me the privilege of watching you get grown

Jamyla Bennu for lovely unexpected gifts and endless support

Bob and Meg Butterworth for making time to visit our crazy house despite living in Seattle

Nakia Scott for keeping me in her prayers

Nadira Goldsmith for inspiring me

Sandra and Nick Merceir for unconditional love and being Mom-mom and Pop-pop

Richard and Dionne Tyler for being the unofficial president of the Shawne Johnson fan club and for always listening and supporting without judgment

Robert Mitchell for being Pop-pop and loving my daughters

The Philadelphia Regional High School and all my teachers (Brian, Mrs. Armstrong, Dr. Keith Rhodes, Douglass Wilde, Ms. Claudette) for giving me a second chance

Dimarco and Dana Garnett for their example of kindness and generosity.

Donald Wharton for being the big brother that I have always wanted

My agent, Jimmy Vines and my editor, Laurie Chittenden for sticking with me these past few years

And my daughters, Zola and Maya, for simply being mine

Shawne Johnson was born and raised in Philadelphia, Pennsylvania, where she now lives with her husband and two daughters. She received her undergraduate degree from Bennett College in Greensboro, North Carolina, and completed her master's degree in English literature at Temple University in Philadelphia. She was also a United States Peace Corps volunteer in Mozambique, Africa, and is the author of *Getting Our Breath Back*. *Eden, Ohio* is her second novel.